I0691509

Mamie's Mayhem

Mamie's Mayhem by
The1Essence

First Printing

ISBN-13: 978-0615842790
(The1Essence_Presentations)

ISBN-10: 0615842798

Acknowledgements

I would like to thank each and every one of you reading this for purchasing of this book. It has been a long time coming for many of you and, I thank you for your patience. Hopefully, this story will excite your imagination and allow your mind to absorb the reality that behind the smile of every ordinary woman, there is an extraordinary life!

Dedication

This book is dedicated to my loved ones in loving memory of
Bryant Ivory Pierce

Yesterday...

Mamie's Mayhem by
The1Essence

...Mamie was tired.

She lay her head back against the supple, softness of the lambskin head rest in Nicole's new, custom made, snow white Lamborghini and, allowed the strength of the ganja she had just inhaled to lull her into a coma like sleep…

"Ja'miah Mee'licent Ba'teest!" Lissette yelled. "A pop'rly mannnered young la'die does not sit like 'dat!"

Jahmiah jumped up from the curb she had been sitting on watching the parade, with her long legs stretched wide open forming a "V" on the litter stained street.

"Ma'maan", she sternly stated as she turned to face her mother standing on the weather worn porch, "I have asked you not to call me by that name anymore! Please Ma'maan, call me Mamie! All of that pomp and circumstance of the old ways is just not my waay!"

Without waiting for a response from the old woman with a face as worn looking as the porch, Mamie stomped down the street behind the rest of the Maris Gras revelers in search of the next parade, while twirling her long, wavy black hair in a bun to bring some relief from the unusually warm weather.

Mamie's Mayhem by
The1Essence

Lissette sighed deeply watching the youngest of her four daughters defiantly march down the street. As she turned to look at the entrance of the old single family row house. She had taken in laundry, sold countless sweet potato pies, and still worked from dawn to dusk caring for the wealthy families in the Garden District, all the while hiding every dime from her gambling thirsty husband, to buy it mortgage free, nearly 20 years ago; her heart was heavy.

Mamie was the last of her children living in her home. Her other daughter's had adhered to Lissettes' guidance and married soon after finishing normal school but, not Mamie. The youngest child of Paul and Lissette Batiste was the most rebellious and not likely to marry because of it.

Lissette worried about the trouble that child was sure to bring back home with her when she returned. She grabbed the old tattered, straw broom and thought of sending Mamie to live in Jackson, MS., with her oldest daughter Catherine and her husband. But, they had just welcomed the birth of their third child and, Lissette was sure that with all Mamie's rambunctious ways, she would most certainly be a burden to them. Paulette and Patrice were both newly weds and with little to no patience for their stubborn sister so; their homes were not an option.

Lissette groaned as she plopped into the creaking rocking chair her husband had made her as a wedding gift so many years ago.
"No," she spoke aloud as she shook her head from side to side. "I will have to see 'dees one to 'de end."

Mamie walked for hours until she found herself standing at the gate to the ferry at the mouth of the great Mississippi River. She watched others board a rather large boat that would take them from the West End of New Orleans to the celebratory, bustling downtown.

"I need to get away from here", she thought when she handed the Captain her fare, still following the crowd.

New Orleans was full of rich history and captivating scenery. But, it was just as full of cunning criminals and, devastating poverty. Only the well manicured Garden District held owners with money, old money that would never settle in the hands of the poor fatherless daughter of a maid like she.

Mamie had never had the pleasure of meeting her father. Well, at least she didn't remember meeting him. He was killed in an alley not far from the partying talking place at this moment on Bourbon Street, when she was still an infant.

Catherine told her, Paul's friends had carried his body on the ferry as if he were merely intoxicated then, put his hat over his face and left him where he sat, when it was time to depart. Lissette searched for him for a week before one of their wives broke her silence and told Lissette of her beloved's fate.

Mamie's Mayhem by
The1Essence

By the time Lissette made it to the morgue, they had already cremated Paul Batiste's body. All that remained of him were a few ashes in a small cardboard box, no bigger than a shoe box marked *"John Doe"*, the date he was cremated and, his blood stained hat.

And, that is how Lissette identified her husbands' remains; by a hat she had only two weeks before, given him for his fiftieth birthday.

None of Mamie's sisters ever had anything good to say about Paul Batiste out of earshot of Lissette. Although Catherine was the eldest, Paulette and Patrice had equally horrifying stories to tell of their father, despite being only six and four years old respectfully, at the time of his death. They all agreed he was a drunkard, a gambler and a cheat. But, most of all, he was a disrespectful, broken man who beat his wife in front of and, cursed his children.

"That man brought ma'maan nothing but hardships and heartbreak", Patrice would whisper at night while Lissette would be ironing the laundry she'd taken on to feed her family.

"When I get married", Paulette whined some nights, "I'm going to change my last *and* my first name!"

"Oh, you must!" Patrice would agree, "To carry the name of such an awful being for eternity is nothing but a curse!"

"She will do no such thing!" Catherine would interrupt when she caught Pauline talking that way.

"But, you saw most, and you knew him best," the tiny Mamie defended Pauline, "you have even said yourself we are all better off now."

"I did see, I did say, and I still do say it's so" Catherine replied, "but, what I know best is that ma'maan loved him dearly, and it is she who gave us all the names we carry! None of you will do anything to disrespect or hurt ma'maan; which will be the exact result of what Pauline will do if she changes her name." The room would become quiet at the mentioning of further burdening Lissettes heart.

"Now, please go to sleep", Catherine pleaded, "I have to help ma'maan finish the ironing and she keeps stopping to ask what could be so important to do so much whispering about"…

Mamie's Mayhem by
The1Essence

All of the Batiste women would take turns helping Lissette with the washing she took in to make extra money and with the cooking and, cleaning around the house.

The first thing to be done after school was homework. Lissette would fly into an unnatural fury if she found out one of the girls was behind in her studies. For it was of the upmost priority for a woman to be of assistance to her husband and, to be able to have a conversation with him after *his* long day of work about something other than the children and *her* day. Or, so Lissette believed.

After home work, it was time to wash the piles of clothes Lissette had carried home during her lunch break then, cook the family's dinner, dust the house and, scrub the floors and bathroom with bleach.

Lissette insisted the girls be efficient in house work and cooking an edible meal. For what use were you to a man if you couldn't prepare him a good meal and keep his house clean? It wasn't good enough to do one thing well and not the other. Not being efficient in both left room for your husband eyes to wander to what another woman could possibly do better.

The girls worked well together around the house, often helping each other with various chores and studies. This pleased Lissette immensely, helping ease the pain of her own traumatic marriage and, soothe any bitterness towards her deceased husband that may start to swell insider her.

"Women only have two options", she would tell her daughters; "you can either be a good wife or a bad woman. *I* was a good wife! What will *your* choice be?"

Mamie's favorite responsibility was baking pastries and cakes to sell to church goers', downtown after Sunday mass.

She had gotten so good at baking, that her sweets were regularly requested by women across the Parish to serve to their families after Sunday dinner and for dinner parties.

Occasionally, the Batiste Girls as they had come to be known; were allowed brief excursions into downtown New Orleans outside of selling bakery but, only together and only, after all studies and chores had been completed.

Each of the girls was allowed to court young men on the porch of their shotgun home when they turned 17. Lissette felt that was old enough to begin setting their sites on a *marrying* man and, showcase what they had to offer *him*. During this courtship, they were not, under any circumstances allowed to leave the porch.

The daughter who was expecting a well screened suitor, baked cookies, pies and other sweets to show the young man that they knew their way around the kitchen. But, there was of course, as with all young couples, the occasional peck on the cheek and, if her sister's could keep Lissette occupied long enough, a quick kiss goodbye on the lips!

When her sisters began getting married and moving away, Mamie started changing. She no longer took pride in her daily routine. Every chore seemed to draw more of her energy away from experience the happiness of life.

More of the responsibilities began to fall on her and, before long; they were all hers and, Mamie started to feel as though she were suffocating every time she climbed the rickety stairs to the old house.

After Patrice married and moved to Texas with her new husband last year, Mamie became distraught. She knew she was expected to finish high school and find a husband of her own to start a family with. But, Mamie had other plans. She wanted to travel! The thought of riding the subways of New York and the A-

Train in Chicago sent thrilling chills up her spine.

Fine men, fast cars, house parties and expensive clothes were on her agenda; not scrubbing floors and clothes until her hands were raw or, cooking and cleaning up behind an unappreciative brood of children, nor was lying under a man who couldn't understand her or possibly appreciated her mind and, would maybe even abuse her body as her father did Lissette's.

No, her sister's could have the family life. Mamie wanted the fast life! And, she thought she knew well that she would have to travel up North to find it!

"When it comes down to it", Mamie thought as she stepped off the ferry, "I've only got one life and I'm going to live it the way I want to! If that means my only option is too be branded a bad woman, well, I'm gonna show 'em just how *baaad*, bad can be!"

Mamie continued to follow the party seekers from the ferry to Bourbon Street where, Fat Tuesday revelry was in full swing! People hung from the balconies over shops, bars and restaurants in costumes and masks dangling beads and tossing coin to the crowd below from one hand while holding tightly to exotic beverages in the other. The crowed slowly moved down the narrow corridor with a joyous spirit in an almost entranced state.

Screams of excitement and drunkenness permeated the air with and eroticism that made Mamie's 16 year old heart race!

"This is what life is about", Mamie thought, "happiness, and celebrations of existence. Not toil, doom and gloom!"

To Mamie, Lissettes way of life was not living at all. And, the life she insisted her daughters lead was just another form of bondage; modern day slavery, truth be told. Mamie chuckled at the thought of the word "truth".

"Tell 'da truf and shame 'da davil", Lissette would often tell her daughters.

As Mamie amused herself at her mother's expense, the massive crowd suddenly surged forward, both pushing and pulling Mamie in opposite directions as the same time. She stumbled then fell, covering her head with her hands; an effort to prevent herself from being trampled.

Mamie squirmed and twitched back and forth on the filthy pavement trying to protected her head and avoid as many feet stomping the rest of her body as she could, for what seemed like an eternity before she felt the space begin to clear around her.

Mamie's Mayhem by
The1Essence

"Hey, hey, watch it", she heard a male voice yell, "there's a little girl down here!"

A strong arm wrapped around her midsection and pulled her into a standing position.

"I ain't a little girl"! Mamie yelled at her rescuer while she dusted herself off.

"Well, I sure can't tell that by the way you were rolling around in the street", the voice laughingly replied

"Ain't shit funnn…" Mamie stopped trying to slap the dirt and grime off her clothes and looked up. Suddenly unable to finish her sentence, she found herself staring into the darkest eyes she had ever seen.

Intrigued she allowed her eyes to take in the full features of the man who had just saved her from being trampled to death but the drunken partiers.

At first glance this man appeared to be White. He had a pale, almost white complexion, pointy nose that seemed to only compliment his dark, mysterious eyes and a full head of silky smooth, wavy, jet black hair.

"What was that little girl?" The man asked the seemingly mesmerized Mamie.

"I, I said, thank-you."

"Well, now, that's not what I thought I heard but, I do think it is the appropriate thing to say, all things considered", he told her.

His voice was deep and soft. Not boisterous and loud, like the voices of the boys at school. Mamie wanted to say something to him to keep him talking to her but; all she could manage to do was stutter more.

"I, I, I'm not a little girl", she stated softly, "I'm almost 18 years old, and I can take care of myself."

The young man, who appeared to be no older than her let out a roaring laugh that stopped just short of hysteria.

"From the looks of things, you are *not* doing a good job of that", he stated with a huge smile on his face. "You'd better hurry home to yo' mammy before you gets hurt out here tryin' to be grown!"

Mamie became incensed at the thought of him making fun of her when, he didn't even know her.

"Look mista', I don'e tol' you thank-you and, I think fo' yo' own sake you betta take that and move on!"

This statement only seemed to further amuse the young man whose laughter mingled with the cheers and screams of the Fat Tuesday celebrators. Mamie's temper and nose began to flare.

"I may be a small strap of leather but I'm well put together so, jump frog!" Mamie's stood directly in front of him with legs spread defensively, one hand on her hip and the other hand sliding into the back pocket of her jeans to make sure the razorblade she had hidden there was still intact.

"Come on Daddie", a sultry voice crooned behind the young man, "she ain't worth nothin', just a piece po' trash."

A young scantly clad and heavily made up woman with a rainbow colored afro, sprinkled with glitter, appeared next to the man; grabbing his arm tightly to show Mamie they were indeed together. The woman could have easily passed for 25 years old so Mamie didn't quite get the relationship between the two.

Mamie and the woman locked eyes. For a short time not a word was said but, it was clear to the young man the women were indeed having a conversation. He grabbed his companion's hand and slowly removed it from his arm, turning his attention to her.

"Since when is it yo' business to concern yo' self with my comins' and goins'?" He calmly almost soothingly spoke to her. "Do I need to publically remind you what yo' concerns *should* be?" He almost whispered.

"No Daddie", the woman replied, dropping her head to stare at her four inch heeled, gold sandals.

"Ey' got 'me erbs nd em rid'dy to git 'ome!"

The heads of Mamie, the young man and what had become clear to Mamie, was his whore, jerked to the left to see an elderly woman standing on the sidewalk yelling towards the couple.

Mamie was in awe of the beauty the old woman still clearly possessed. Her snow white hair had been cut in the popular pageboy style of the day. She resembled Florence Ballard of the Supremes, only old. The old woman banged the bottom of her cane hard against the ground twice.

"Nicodemus! Ey' don 'ave the stomach for dis 'ere crowd 'o mad'ness, so let's git ta gittin'!" Then she turned and began pushing people to the side with her cane, maneuvering though the crowd.

A smile grew across Mamie's dirt stained face; "Nicodemus, huh?" She said as she looked into his suddenly frowning face. He looked at her and smiled back.

"Yeah", he replied, "But, you can call me Cutty, the next time we meet." Then he grabbed the whore by her elbow and led her off into the crowd behind the old woman.

"Not in this lifetime!" Mamie yelled behind him and, started through the crowd in the opposite direction.

Mamie half stumbled, half pushed her way through the crowd. She had enough of avoiding Lissette's scorn for the day and decided to head home. Even the Mardi Gras festivities were becoming a bore to her. Moreover, that revelation fueled the fire to escape the sorrowful incarceration of the South for the brazen defiance of self freedom waiting for her up North.

Mamie decided to pick up a few warm beignets, and coffee to cheer her mother up, she knew Lissette would still be brooding over their last exchange. Mamie had in fact been disrespectful to her and felt sorry for those words.

Her path to Café Du Monde from Bourbon Street took Mamie through a familiar alleyway filled with ghastly memories of innocents lost. She could have avoided this way altogether but, fear was no longer an emotion Mamie gave credence to.

As she walked through the dirty ally filled with empty boxes, crates and spattered with unmentionable filth, Mamie once again eased her hand into the comfort of the rear pocket of her jeans, grasping the security of her sharp razorblade handle.
She remembered, being in the same place only two short years ago.

She remembered the darkness of the alleyway on that fateful night. She even remember the joy she felt as she skipped and smiled to herself, knowing how much the coins in her pockets from the sale of her baked goods would make Lissette. Even then, caution and fear had no place in Mamie's psyche. The only thoughts dancing around in her mind were of replacing Lissette's pain of her increasing empty home, two days after Patrice's wedding with an ear to ear grin.

It wasn't until she felt the pain of someone grabbing a fist full of her hair. And, smelled the foul breath of a drunken man's breath against her cheek did fear set it. The terror of the atrocities that followed were buried under the surface of Mamie's skin deep enough that pain didn't show on her face but not enough to erase the scars in her mind.

Mamie wanted revenge on her attackers, which is why she never hesitated to walk this way when the opportunity presented itself and, always under the protection of a few ever ready, strategically placed razor blades.

She wanted those disgusting creatures masking around in the shells of men to pay. Not for robbing her of an innocence that at this point in her life was not cherished but for making her afraid of the light; for taking something that she did not offer and, for merely existing as frauds in society.

In Mamie's mind these monsters were probably masquerading as, husbands, fathers, and upstanding citizens. And, she would not unmask their charade but she was surely obsessed with the thought of, making them pay with their lives for their exploitation of human trust.

Mamie chuckled at the thought of taking a life. Certainly she didn't classify these men as human but their steady heartbeat mattered to someone.

She had never done so before. But, the connotation did not unnerve her in the least.

Anger, rage and non-repentance had replaced her innocence with a vengeance comparable to being possessed by one of the demons mentioned in the small worn black book of Voodoo spells, hidden under Lissette's mattress. Mamie thought it ironic to have stumbled upon the book early one Sunday morning before Mass.

Lissette often left her handkerchiefs to flatten under the mattress. Leaving them as crisp as a fresh ironing upon removal.

Mamie, in search of a clean, a pressed handkerchief without reprisal for being unprepared for church, discovered the book of spells but, not its importance to Lissette. It was apparent to Mamie then that there was more to her mother than the eye could distinguish.

"Hey pretty Lady! Can I go with you?"

Mamie's reminiscing was interrupted by the voice of a man, who suddenly appeared next to her. The stranger threw his arm around her neck and pulled Mamie close to him, giving the impression to any who may be watching that they were together as a couple.

Mamie's growing inner smile inside quickly bubbled up into laughter that escaped her mouth as she pulled her hand out of her pocket, swung her hand towards his face in a forged motion of a caress and drug the razor blade down the side of the strange man's cheek. The man pushed Mamie away from him.

"You bitch!" He yelled at Mamie, grabbing his profusely bleeding cheek as she continued laughing at him.

Mamie's Mayhem by
The1Essence

While steadying her stance in preparation to strike again; Mamie's laughter increases to a bewitching cackle. She swung death her equipped her right arm at the man again. Mid swing she heard galloping horse hooves. An urgency for vigilantly increased her heartbeat and she struck him again on the opposite cheek, this time taking the time to enjoy the feeling of the spitting flesh and the spurting blood as she dug deeper into his face.

"Arrrgggggh! I' ma kill you Bitch!" Mamie's unsuspecting victim yelled, lunging at her with both now bloody hands. Mamie jumped back, avoiding his attack on her and lashed her arm out again, slashing his forehead.

The sound of hooves approached at a faster pace now. The mounted officer yelled "STOP!", at Mamie until he was close enough to jump off of the horse and land in front of her, separating the victim from certain doom.

"Arrest that crazy bitch! She tried to kill me", the stranger yelled at Officer Benton.

Facing Mamie with both arms spread to ward off any further attacks, Officer Benton turned to his head slightly to the side towards the man.

"You disgust me! You are lucky I don't run you in!" he spat. "Your motives were a whole hell of a lot less honorable than hers!

Mamie's Mayhem by
The1Essence

Now get out of her before I step aside and let her end your miserable existence!"

The man picked himself off the ground and ran off into an adjourning alleyway as the police officer turned his attention back to Mamie.

Officer Benton looked into Mamie's dark eyes and studied her heaving chest. No one could convince him that he was not standing in front of the most beautiful woman he had ever laid eyes of or, the most dangerous. For he knew the dark secret behind those huge captivating doe eyes and, he knew that secret kept this young woman drowning in a soul burning in turmoil.

"Mamie", he whispered toward her, "Let's calm down, please", he pleaded, reaching out to her. "Let me take you home, this is not the one of the men who hurt you."

"Fuck you!" Mamie spat at him. "You know what he wanted! You know what he was going to try to do to me! I won't, I can't let that happen to me or anyone else again!"

"I know, I know that but, he's gone now and, I, I'm here. "Come on, and let him be. It's time to go home." He told her, still trying to calm her down and restore a tiny bit of her sanity.

Mamie's Mayhem by
The1Essence

Mamie's eyes soften and she took a step toward Officer Benton. He reached out, grabbed her and pulled her to his chest hugging her with both of his arms as tightly as he could. How he wished he could always be around to protect her. And, longing for a day when she would willingly hug him back.

Burying his head in her long, think hair, Officer Benton pulled Mamie closer, close enough to smell the scent of jasmine permeating from her locks.

"Come on, let me help you onto Stella and take you home", he whispered in her ear.

Mamie moved with his help onto the waiting horse, as if she where emerging from a 20 year coma. Completely shaken and engulfed by the dark, murkiness of the alleyway.

Unbeknownst, to both Mamie and Officer Benton, a car occupied by three spectators, sat at the end of the alley, with its occupants watching the entire scene unfold in complete silence, until now.

"Wow! That alley cat sure knows how to handle her business! And, to think, I was worried about her safety!" Cutty broke the ice cold silence of the car with his astonishment.

"*Un chat de gouttière avec l'âme dangereux combats d'une panthère*", (An alley cat with the dangerous fighting soul of a

Mamie's Mayhem by
The1Essence

panther), Cutty's platinum haired mother, Nicolette McGillicuddy replied.

"That one will be on top, no matter the circumstance. Now, let us leave here. We have a home to attend to", Nicolette commanded her son with almost a sinister grunt.

Cutty started the engine and slowly moved down the street toward the highway as Rachel fidgeted in the back seat, adjusting her itchy wig and scratching her head, thinking this alley cat carried the stank of trouble that must be reported to her twin sister Ruby right away!

Officer Benton wanted to prolong his moments with Mamie as long as possible so he and his horse Stella accompanied her on the ferry from New Orleans to the city's West Bank. He held her as close as she would let him as she went through mental fits of quiet rage. Sometimes looking up at him, gritting her teeth and pushing him away. Only to grab his hand moments later and allowing him to pull her back into his tight embrace.

"God, if only she would let me shine just a little light in her dark space, I know I could make her happy", he prayed on one such occasion when Mamie allowed him in close.

The ferry moved with quiet stealth across the Mississippi River. The smell emerging from its imposing depths evoked a two year old memory in both Mamie and Officer Benton of events uncannily like those of this evening. Only the outcome was gravely different…

On an evening much like this one. When the entire City of New Orleans seemed not to have a care in the world other than celebrating, Officer Thaddeus Benton was just ending his shift in the downtown area of the City. It was almost 8pm and darkness has settled on the city swiftly, bringing with it an unusual thick odor that made Thad sent shivers down Thad's spine. On nights like these, Thad's mom, a Haitian immigrant, would say the Devil was setting fires to souls on earth and there was something evil sure to appear with the sunrise.

He decided to walk his new patrol horse in to the station to temporarily relieve her of the weight his 6'4, 225lb. frame surely burdened her with for the last 9 hours. And, even though his shift was over, he wanted to make one more round through the dangerous alleys of New Orleans that were saturated with pick pockets, hustlers, prostitutes and worse.

Thad had just entered the last alley on his way to the station when he thought he heard a scream about two blocks down.

Mamie knew she shouldn't walk down the alley but, it was the fastest way to Café' Du Monde where she wanted to pick up a few beignets to dissipates Lissette's wedding blues

acquired by Patrice's wedding and departure
from their home just two days before.

She skipped and laughed at how she knew
Lissette would elate at the fact that all of the
pastries were sold and there would be money
for wood to warm the house this week. It
wasn't until she felt the pain of someone
grabbing a fist full of her hair. And, smelled
the foul breath of a drunken man's breath
against her cheek that she realized she had
made a mistake. Her attacker was fast and
aggressive despite his obvious overweight
body, and he wasn't alone.
There was another skinny man with him and
they both reeked of filth and alcohol.

The fat man rammed Mamie's head into
the cold brick of the back of a nearby building.
Now holding her by the neck so tightly she
could not scream he forced her leg apart and
ripped her underwear from underneath the
checkered skirt she wore as part of her school
uniform.

"Oh yeah," he snorted to his accomplice,
"This cherry is ripe and ready!" He forced her
head from the wall into the filthy cobblestone
alley floor.

Mamie gasped for air then let out a
piercing scream that was lost in the cheers of
Beal Street partiers as the more aggressive of

her attackers forced himself into her from behind and began to brutally sodomize her.

"Here!" he barked to his coconspirator without stopping his inhumane stabs, "put this in her mouth!"

Mamie's eyes bulged out of her head when she recognized the torn rags as remnants of her favorite white underpants. They were quickly shoved into her mouth, preventing her from expressing the agonizing pain of the vicious rape.

"Naw Boy," the accomplice rethought his actions, "I got something for that purty mouth of hers!"

He unzipped his pants, reaching in and pulling out a tiny but obviously erect penis resembling half eaten corn dog. With one swift motion removed the rags from Mamie's mouth and replaced it with midget member.

The pain from being sodomized and the stench emitting from the crotch being shoved back and forth in her face with two fists full of hair, made Mamie's stomach and blood boil! She closed her eyes tightly and allowed the falling tears to lull her spirit to sleep.

Her rapists, lost in the grunts and groans of their heinous acts did not notice that their victim had fallen unconscious. Nor, did they hear the sound of hooves rushing toward them.

Mamie's Mayhem by
The1Essence

"*Hey! Hey, what's going on there?*"
Officer Benson screamed at the two, possibly three, figures in the shadows of the alley. At realization of what was taking place, and without response from the shadowed figures, he quickened the pace of the trotting horse into a full gallop towards the crime.

The thinner of the assailants, who was very close to bringing his pleasure to an explosive release, was interrupted by the screaming Officer Benson.

"*Scat Cat*", *he yelled at his partner who, immediately his coma like trance.*

"*SHIT!*" *Fatty screamed.*

The simultaneous release of Mamie's body by both of the men sent her body crashing, full force into the grimy we cobblestone. The attackers ran in opposite directions, leaving the furious officer to decide which of the two pursue. He instead chose to focus his attention on Mamie's half clothed, slight frame, now lying face down on the ground in a pool of vomit.

Thad cradled the still unconscious young girl in his arms, and walked by to the nearby ally apartment of a known whore, with Stella obediently trailing behind him. He banged on the door a couple of times with his foot until a scantily clad woman with disheveled hair opened the door.

"What is it, I'm in my own apartment doing nothing wrong!" The woman said sternly as she peeked from behind the chained door.

"Open the door, I need your help!" Thad replied.

Noticing the officer had a little girl in his arms; the whore quickly released the chain and swung the door open.

"What have you done? Does Madam Nicolette know that you are here?" She worriedly spoke.

The whore occupied a tiny studio apartment. Only a worn brass bed and a dusty wooden dresser furnished the room that also had an unflattering wood floor that creaked like an old pirate ship. A small bathroom attached to the makeshift bedroom was the only other space in the apartment.

"No! And, I need you to go to the bar down the street and call her right away", Thad yelled at her as he lay Mamie's body on the tussled mattress that sagged in the middle.

"Go now, no more questions!"

Thad belted out his last command so forcibly that the startled whore jump to grab her shawl and left the room without making another sound.

Once alone with the young girl, Thad could only sit on the edge of the bed and hold her hand. He gazed at her, grief stricken as if she was his own sister.

Only God would be able to heal her psychological wounds but he hoped his mother could clean her up well enough for him to take her home to her family with the least discourse.

He knew he should have taken her to the hospital, in fact his job required that he do just that. Mamie stirred but did not wake.

Thad felt helpless as he waited for Nicolette to arrive. As he studied Mamie's face, he could not help but notice how beautiful her lips were. They appeared so full and soft, despite the apparent bruising and cut on the upper lip.

Overcome by a searing attraction, Thad bent over to kiss Mamie. He was close enough to smell her breath emanating vomit when he heard the doorknob turn and the imposing force that embodied Nicolette McGillicuddy emerged in the doorway with her whore following close behind.

Mamie's Mayhem by
The1Essence

Nicolette

Mamie's Mayhem by
The1Essence

Nicolette McGillicuddy was born Nicolette Aristie, a Haitian immigrant that migrated to the United States to escape the poverty and oppression of Francois "Daddy Doc" Duvalier.

Unbeknownst to all, Nicolette was in the U.S., illegally. However, no one within the confines of New Orleans was bold enough to challenge her on her citizenship.

Nicolette stood 5"11 and was almost as wide as she was tall. She kept her bleached blond hair wrapped tightly, in a black or white turban with only a small partition hanging out of the front of it, and a large, wooden walking stick with a skull, bones and crosses carved into it only minutely interrupted her gait.

Still, her arresting stature was one that held undeniable beauty, which had seen better days.

Her ebony skin was smooth as satin and, her large haunting eyes held the purest white. Matching her perfect teeth, teeth, which were only visible when she threw her head, back to release a bloodcurdling cackle; a laugh, which could be heard many echoing for miles around the Parish.

On first glance, Nicolette was a loving doting grandmother. To a stranger upon making her acquaintance she was the mother of her community.

During her life in America, Nicolette had built a wholesome reputation by taking in young women who society had thrown in the street to rid themselves of any impurity, feeding the sick, homeless and supplying housekeeping jobs to any "stray" young lady in need of income and a warm, safe place to rest; anyone who was unfamiliar with the name her nickname "Madame Obscurit'e" or "Madam Darkness" welcomed her presence.

The reality of Nicolette's reputation was exactly the opposite. Nicolette did absolutely nothing that did not benefit her financially. Even the birth of her two boys came with a price tag to their fathers.

Moreover, the most intimidating aspect of Nicolette's life was her practice of the Voodoo religion. Rumors in the various Parishes did not deviate far from fact. Many said that just a menacing glance from the self-proclaimed Voodoo Priestess could cause you heart to stop or, at the very least, could cause your child to develop a severe case of hives.

Despite gruesome and often exaggerated rumors', Politicians, law enforcement officers and the grimiest of cut throat criminals came to

Nicolette for fortune telling, Voudo cures, advice and to indulge in her hospitality.

Nicolette's hospitality referred to the services, mostly sexual in nature, offered by young wayward and homeless girls she'd coerced off the streets with promise of a safe place to sleep, warm surroundings, a hot meal and promises of the opportunity to become a part of the wealthy, elite and revered New Orleans population. Everyone in the Parish knew of the things that went on in Madame Darkness' home, yet never a negative ward was publically uttered in fear of her casting a voodoo spell on the perpetrator or one of their beloved family members. She commanded a regime almost and feared as the one she fled in Haiti.

When the younger, slimmer Nicolette arrived in New Orleans, she met and married a young maluatto farmer name, Richard Benton. He was captivated by her silky skin, long thick black hair, and alluring voice and she was obsessed with marriage to a man of means.

For a while, married life suited her, Richard worked his farm during the day. He had enough land to afford hired farm hands, which left Nicolette to their farmhouse and only occasionally wonder into New Orleans to shop for household items.

Mamie's Mayhem by
The1Essence

Eventually she became bored with the daily routine of a farmer's wife. There was something more this world had to offer her and but she couldn't but her finger on what she was missing. By all accounts she lived a charmed and wealthy life compared to those she left behind in Haiti. And, her doting husband became more devoted once she gave birth to their son.

But, the birth of the child only made Nicolette feel suffocated. So, she started a prayer group for the wives of farmers who had Haitian background.

They sang hymns on Sunday morning, well into the afternoon, studied the Bible on Wednesday nights and indulged in the ritualistic Kanzo rites, practice of Voudo on Saturday night. Nicolette quickly became the Mambos (Female Voudo Priest) of their Sect.

Shortly after becoming Mambos, some say be a cunning show of force, threats and bribes other say by casting spells so menacing she no one dared vote against, the young Mrs. Benton, Nicolette became bored with being the wife of a sugarcane farmer. She began to whine and tempt her husband to brute force.

She berated his ability to provide for his family as she and their son only had the bare necessities when his money could afford much more. But, Richard was very frugal man.

He has watched his family before him struggle, become wealthy only to lose it all to gluttony. He would not budge in his stronghold of the household finances. But, he did allow Nicolette to seek employment. Thus, she went to work keeping house for Patrick McGillicuddy, a wealthy local restaurateur, toting her infant son with her on a sack on her back while she worked.

Soon after beginning work for Mr., & Mrs., McGillicuddy, Mr. McGillicuddy's young Irish bride became deathly ill and died of stomach cancer in their home with Nicolette by her side crying and carrying on about her "Madam".

After his wife's death, Mr. McGillicuddy leaned on Nicolette to help him through the emotionally draining recovery. Nicolette began spending more time at work, often arriving home well after midnight, smelling of alcohol, rising before dawn and departing just as the new day broke through the clouds.

This did not sit well with Richard. He was a proud man from a family of farmers that scorned a woman's work outside the home. Yet, his desire to hold on to every penny the farm made him allow that rule to be broken with conditions. Now, his wife was not spending anytime at home or tending his needs. Even worse, his son was being raised away from him in the presence of a White man. Richard told Nicolette there would be no more work outside their home one evening and a physical fight ensued.

Rumor throughout the Parrish is that the neighbors closest to them, five miles away could hear Mr. Benton screaming for mercy and by morning any trace of Nicolette, with exception of her young son Thaddeus had been completely erased from the farm.

Nicolette was once heard telling someone "if it wasn't for the life of that sweet babe, that Negro would be DEAD! Voudo has the opposite effect on those you bear children with. I would be the damned of the damned"!

When Nicolette arrived at the home of Patrick McGillicuddy before dawn on that fateful night, she played the victim. She cried and carried on about how in a jealous rage, Richard had beaten her and thrown her out of the house, forbidding her to ever see her son again.

Patrick McGillicuddy turned beat red with anger! How dare that darky believe he had rights to anything! Nicolette begged Patrick to let the situation stand as it was. She only needed a place to lay her head for a short while until she could find residence elsewhere. Nicolette knew she was playing with Patrick's pride. She'd heard him ranting and raving about the rights Blacks in America "thought" they deserved.

"The whole entire Country is going to Hell in a hand basket", she'd heard him expel in a drunken rant.

She also knew Patrick had visited the bordello quite a bit since his wife died and his drinking had increase also.

Nicolette was happy she was done with Richard; she would reclaim her child eventually. That was not an issue and, her growing reputation as a Mambo would ensure that. That very day she set in motion a plan to marry Patrick McGillicuddy.

A White man in an open relationship with a Black woman was absolutely unheard of during at this time in New Orleans!

This feat would prove to be the greatest of all Nicolette's New Orleans legends and solidify her place atop the local Voudo communities.

When Patrick left for his restaurant that morning, Nicolette began the Lover Voudo ritual. Anointing herself with oils, sprinkling the house with the same oils and inundating every room with incense while chanting the lover's prayer. The drunken Patrick came home to a freshly bathed, oiled and scantily clad Nicolette in his parlor.

Whether it was the intoxication from the several shots of brandy he had consumed before arriving home or the lovers spell allure by Nicolette will never be told but, from that moment on, Patrick McGillicuddy was infatuated with everything Nicolette.

He showered her with expensive jewelry and clothing. They spent romantic weekends at the Château his family owned just outside of the city limits. His friends and family could not figure out what had come over their overtly racist relative but, after hearing through their savants' of Nicolette's religious accomplishments, they dared not interfere.

Three months later, Nicolette tearfully told Patrick that she was pregnant. Feigning fear of being ostracized by her community and reported by her estranged husband to immigration officials, then sent back to Haiti with child, Nicolette fell on her knees and crying and pleading her for her "Master" Patrick's help.

Totally taken by the emotional exclamation of undying servitude, Patrick McGillicuddy proclaimed no harm would come to his unborn child or his new wife; and, that was precisely what Nicolette had known he would do.

The next morning, Patrick had papers for divorce formally served to Richard Benton without protest. Thirty days later Nicolette was Mrs. Patrick McGillicuddy, to the horror of the McGillicuddy clan. Now it was time for the Patrick's family to take a stand! Voudo priestess or not, their family could not be disgraced in their new country as they had been in the old.

Before Patrick's first wife died, he had commissioned a small chateau near the Oak Alley Plantation as a surprise anniversary gift to her. Since she didn't live to see its completion, he gifted the deed to Nicolette as a wedding present. They spent their two weeks of their married life at their new vacation home where Patrick allowed Nicolette to spare no expense in its decoration. Nicolette believed she had finally gained the wealth and the status she knew she was destined to have, and likewise gave no mind to sparing expense for the chateau's adornment.

Each evening of their honeymoon vacation, the new Mrs. McGillicuddy would lite candles, incense and bath in the master bedroom's extra wide bathtub. Once she her body was cleansed by a mixture of raw sugar and calamine extract, she would rub her ebony skin with helping hands and rose oil, reciting Psalms 23 until her body glistened and felt like lambskin to the touch. Then she would call her husband to bed. Pleasing him in ways once unimaginable to him until sleep pried him from her grasp.

Meanwhile, the McGillicuddy clan had set into motion a plan to save the reputation of their family and rid themselves of the mangy Negro that had brought them disgrace. Led my Patrick's younger sister Emily, who still cherished the memory of his one and only wife, as far as she was concerned, calls were made to the Parish Constable, Judge and asylum. The family had Patrick declared legally insane and prepared to have him committed to the asylum immediately upon his return to New Orleans.

The new Mr. and Mrs. McGillicuddy returned to their home after two weeks of lethargic bliss. Patrick had arranged for a horse drawn carriage to take them the 30 miles into the city in effort to extend the almost dreamlike honeymoon until the last possible moment. For once the sun rose on the next day he would once again be consumed by the day to day goings on at his restaurant.

It was shortly before sunset when the carriage stopped in front of their modest Garden home. Both Patrick and Nicolette and were greeted by Emily and the Constable La Junne in front of the house. Nicolette grabbed Patrick's arm and began to cry.

"I knew the happiness wouldn't last. They have come to murder my child"! Nicolette exclaimed to the confused Patrick.

"Nonsense!" Patrick replied. "There may have been a problem at the restaurant. Calm yourself, for the baby's sake."

Patrick stopped the carriage driver and jumped out, walking toward the two people standing on his porch, leaving Nicolette in the carriage.

"I don't suppose you two are here to congratulate me?" He stated, stopping in front of them. Emily was the first to speak.

"Patrick, you must know that this sham of a marriage is not valid! You must know the turmoil you have caused this family with your shenanigans"!

"Shenanigan's? Family?" Patrick yelled at her stepping closer to his sister. Emily gasped and stepped back.

"Sir, I must ask you to calm down!" The constable said as he stepped between the two. "I understand this is a family matter but, the law has been involved and in this Parish, I am the law!"

"So, I am asking you to calm down and step inside so that we can remedy this situation." Patrick stepped back from his two visitors.

"Well, let me just get my wife and our bags and we will definitely remedy this!" Patrick spoke through clenched teeth then turned towards Nicolette who was still sitting in the carriage.

Nicolette had a very strange feeling in her stomach about the scene she watched unfold in front of her. She knew from Emily's visits to the McGillicuddy home, when she was merely the maid that Emily's racism ran deep.

She tried to think of which spell she should have used to ward off this type of incident. She had been too caught up in the euphoria of how well, and quickly her plan had worked that she neglected to think of how Patrick's family would react. And, now it was too late to invoke the Spirits of the dead to aid her. But, no matter the outcome here today, Nicolette thought, Emily would be dealt with for her part in the interference.

Once inside the home, everyone stood in the living room, with the exception of Nicolette who planted her enormous bulging body in one of the cherry wood Queen Anne chairs near the window. Immediately, she noticed the carriage had been replaced with a mule drawn wagon full of her belongings.

"This ends now!" Emily directed her words spoken through clenched teeth towards Patrick but, kept her eyes on Nicolette.

"And I suppose the, *this* you are speaking of is my marriage? You have no say so in what goes on in my life, my home, Emily. Everything I own, is mine outright. Neither you nor anyone else has any authority over me." Patrick returned. Emily turned to the constable.

"You see this! He has gone completely mad! If this is the proof you need, standing before you."

"Proof! Proof of what? That I am a man, very much in charge of my life and, prepared to live it the way I want to!"

"Sir", the constable interrupted, "your family has petitioned the courts to have you declared legally insane. There is a warrant issued for your immediate arrest."

"Arrest? Arrest me for what? Getting married, being a husband to a Negro wife and a father to a Negro child? My God, this *is* New Orleans!" Patrick screamed.

"Sir! I will not ask you to control yourself again!" The constable yelled back. "You are free to make all the Negro bastards you are able! But, it has become clear to me that you do not understand the laws of this land. And, here, no respectable White man my legally make a Negro woman his legal wife. You are a White man aren't you? And, for this matter, your family has taken it upon themselves to stop you from further making a fool of them and yourself!"

Nicolette listened but, watched the activity outside the window more intensely as the sun gave way to a full moon.

She felt like standing in the center of the room and screaming to *Baron La Croix* in reverential prayer to take claim of all in the room save herself and her unborn child. She didn't need any of them. She had the title of "Mrs. McGillicuddy" and, legal paperwork that would provide her and her child all the luxuries she believed she deserved. Still she sat silent and waited patiently for what she knew would come.

Nicolette released her murderous thoughts and returned to her full attention back to the conversation before her. Patrick was in a full rage and two deputies were now standing between him and Emily.

"Emily, how dare you try to take control of my life and business? Let he that is without sin cast the first stone! And, you my dear sister are not without sin!" Patrick roared.

"Sir! Lower your voice, SIR!" One of the deputies yelled back at Patrick. Constable La Junne stepped forward.

"I see and agree with the young Ms. McGillicuddy. You are indeed insane in your thoughts and actions, Patrick. Therefore yo…"

"Therefore you are going to relieve me of my home, my business, and other assets?" Patrick loudly interrupted.

"No Sir, I am not. I am taking you to the hospital to be placed under the observation of a physician until it is determined you have returned to your normal self. Deputies do your job."

Both deputies moved forward in attempt to restrain and remove Patrick from the premises but, before they could cuff him, Patrick began throwing wild punches that landed nowhere. As the men began to physically restrain Patrick, Nicolette stood, still clutching her pocketbook and still, not uttering a sound.

As the three men cuffed and began to drag Patrick from their home Nicolette reached inside her pocketbook and retrieved a small burlap satchel. She squeezed the satchel tightly in her palm until she felt the sharp prick of a broken chicken bone pierce her skin, surely drawing blood that was being quickly absorbed in the bag and, mingling with its contents.

Emily had been watching her brother being dragged from the house screaming and kicking wildly until she realized Nicolette was now standing and staring at her intensely. She turned to the towering Negro woman and, strode superiorly towards her stopping only when she was close enough to see what she thought was fear in Nicolette's eyes before she spoke.

"You will be taking back to the country home. You will be sent a generous monthly stipend for you and the child but, you must never return to this house, it was never meant to be your home."

Nicolette re-versed the frail White woman's stare not uttering a word, while Emily took Nicolette's glassy stare to be not one of defiance but of defeat. So, she continued reproaching the woman.

"I by default am in charge of all of my brother's finances until a medical doctor has deemed him sane enough to return to society. And, even then you nor, that bastard you carry are welcome in this house or this family. My brother will be allowed to keep all my father has given him only if he denounces you and this faux marriage. And, he will be permitted to visit you at the country home but never to acknowledge either of you in the presence of respectable citizens."

Nicolette now released her grip on the satchel where the sweat from her palm has now mingled with her blood to craft a deadly potion. There was just one final act activate its power. There was a deliberate tremor in Nicolette's voice as and she finally spoke, focusing on Emily's widening pupils.

"Baron Samedi Ge-Rouge!" Nicolette spat as she clenched Emily's palm between both her hands tightly.

The sight prick of the satchel's contents into the palm of her hand startled Emily and then sent her into a rage as she struggled to pull away from Nicolette's death grip.

"What is this? More of your Voodoo tricks! I am not afraid! You will NOT intimidate me nor will I be a willing participant like my brother! GET OUT!" Emily screamed.

Nicolette released her hand and, with her held up high and slightly tilted, she sauntered out the front door with a faint smile on her face, not looking back.

"I will not be denied", she gloated as she made her way to the mule drawn wagon.

Mamie's Mayhem by
The1Essence

Inside the house, Emily noticed that the palm of her hand was bleeding. She rushed to the kitchen sink to rinse away the blood then she applied pressure stopping its steady flow. It wasn't until she was home in bed the next morning that she noticed the palm of her hand had begun to itch. The more she scratched the more her palm, then her hand began to itch and, the blackness spread. In a matter of minutes her entire hand was the color of burned bark; then the fever set in....

Upon notification of Emily McGillicuddy's death by scarlet fever the Constable immediately released Patrick from the insane asylum to handle his family affairs, with one stipulation.

"Do not openly engage in relations with that Negro woman. There are rules here Sir that must not be broken."

Patrick fully understood the Constables words. And, now after a few days to reflect on his actions of the past few months, he knew exactly how to rectify the situation. He immediately rode his horse to his country home and informed Nicolette of his regrets and his stance on their relationship. Finding her relaxing on the porch in a rocking chair, he made his point very clear.

"We are no longer publically husband and wife; you will not be addressed or acknowledged as such", he told her, "save for in this domicile."

"You are not to publically acknowledge me in the State of Louisiana as the father of any children we may bring into this world and, never enter my business or any business I may frequent through the front door nor ever question my actions as a White man and a man of means".

"For this discretion, you and your children will be taken care of respectively yet with caution for my stand in this community. Any compromise of these rules will be met with complete abandonment of my obligations financially to you."

Nicolette understood fully and silently agreed with nothing more than a solemn nod of her head. She was not in love with Patrick McGillicuddy so there was no need for continued spectacle. She was still mistress of a household. Something she would never have accomplished in Haiti. And, something she would exert full advantage of in America.

Still, she lamented over a lonely life, absent of a true love and, vanished to the outskirts of New Orleans. Yet, she had status, she had Patrick's money and, she was still a

Voudo Priestess among the Blacks in the Parish. For now, that was all she and her unborn child would need. She would make a name for herself in New Orleans without the love of a man. All she needed was a family. One she would create with the powers of the Wretched Saints. All she needed was the ultimate Air to her empire and, the child she carried would be the key…

As Patrick went about the routine of burying his sister and re-establishing his status in New Orleans, Nicolette set into motion her plan of building an empire of complete domination over anyone showing a weakness of Spirit.

But first her bulging stomach, which prevented her from keeping house, beckoned her to hire a maid and cook. She immediately placed an advertisement in the local newspaper.

Lissette

Mamie's Mayhem by
The1Essence

Lissette Batiste took the ferry from the West Bank of New Orleans to McGillicuddy's Pub and Restaurant in Downtown New Orleans as soon as she saw the advertisement for a maid and kitchen help in the morning newspaper. Although she had an evening job watching Madam Fuse's twins, her husband's gambling habit had gotten out of control and required her to find a second job to make ends meet.

Madam Fuse had been very generous with her salary the last four years. And that generosity had provided the necessary funds to pay off the mortgage on the modest home Lissette and her family lived in. But, now her husband had grown weary of his family and indulged his lust for street life more fervently than he ever had in Haiti. He rarely worked and when he did Lissette had to meet him at the end of his shift to collect his pay or they would have to go without some pertinent need until the next payday.

Her eldest daughter Catherine would have to take on more responsibility and see herself and her sisters Paulette and Pauline off to school and fix their supper. They needed the extra monies and the girls would have to adjust to their mother taking on the role of head of the household.

Mamie's Mayhem by
The1Essence

When Lissette informed Madam Fuse that it was necessary for her to take on another job, Madam did not protest. Mansour Fuse had frequently reported to his wife the adverse goings of Paul Batiste.

She knew Lissette and the girls were in dire straits but, still she informed Lissette that the Fuse children would not have supper late or suffer any way from the added responsibilities or her job in that household would be terminated.

Lissette arrived at McGillicuddy's pub feeling the onset of exhaustion and something else she could not put her finger on. She was ushered toward the back entrance by a young black man out in front of the pub who was sweeping the sidewalk. He told her that the owner was in the kitchen just inside the rear entrance.

As she made her way to the other entrance she gripped her small rosary she held between her gloved hands tightly and, began to recite Psalms 23. Something inside told her that if she got this job her life would change forever. Lissette shook off the bad feelings, finished her prayer and headed down the alley towards the back door yet; she belabored each step down the wet, dirty, cobble stone alley.

Lissette gently tapped three times on a wooden door with tattered screens which was barely attached to the entrance of the rear of the building as she was directed to by the sweeping young man. With each tap her heart seemed to beat just a little slower giving a slight feeling of light headedness. Instantly, a male beckoned her inside.

"Come in."

Patrick McGillicuddy stood inside a cluttered restaurant kitchen at a metal double sink in a dirty black apron and black rubber gloves, washing dishes. He didn't turn around immediately to great the middle aged woman who had quietly entered the room until her soft voice quietly draw him towards it possessor.

"Good morning. I am here to apply for the job you advertised in the newspaper."

Patrick stop washing dishes and turned around to see Lissette timidly standing just inside the back entrance of his pub, tenderly fingering a salt water pearl rosary. Suddenly, he found himself focusing her porcelain like face; more intensely the light pink lips that had just uttered words that now resonated in his head in a foreign language to him. He was entranced by Lissette's beauty and exposed humility. His common sense reminded him of the experience of an interracial relationship with Nicolette and urged him to control his lust but, passion told him he had to have this gentle woman standing in front of him.

Lissette aware of Patrick's lustful stare lowered her eyes to the floor and again inquired about the advertisement.

"Misère, I am here for the job a'vertised in the paper for maid service. I would like to apply."

Embarrassed and startled by the realization that his lustful thoughts had been recognized in his stare, Patrick cleared his throat and forced himself to speak.

"Do you have children?"

"Yes Misère", Lissette timidly responded.

Patrick found confidence in her nervousness and became more direct and poise in his questions, for they now had more purpose than acquiring a maid for Nicolette.

"Please look at me when we speak. This job has is not one for a thin skinned person as the mother of my unborn child revels in dominance. Now, who cares for you children while you are working?"

From that moment on Lissette answered each of Patrick's questions directly and with confidence not forgetting the intensity of his initial stared but with the understanding that she and the girls needed the extra income.

Mamie's Mayhem by
The1Essence

The next morning Patrick arose early at and left the Garden District home he had recently returned, to ferry his Buick across the Mississippi to personally pick Lissette up from her West Bank home; with the purpose of driving her to the Carriage house where his common law wife was waiting on the arrival of her new servant. As he drove Patrick took the opportunity to pry more into the personal life of this woman who had him so enraptured.

To his surprise, Lissette spoke very candidly about her husband drunkenness and gambling problem. Patrick then decided that he would personally drive Lissette to work in the morning to ensure her timely arrival, giving Nicolette one less reason to fire the woman he knew she would become envious of and, also with the hopes of developing a more intimate relationship with Lissette. Nicolette's spells of passion had long since worn off Patrick. Still his desire for women of color remained.

The initial meeting between Nicolette and Lissette went better than Patrick expected. He thought Nicolette would immediately become jealous of Lissette's porcelain doll like facial features and petite body; features exactly opposite of her own, and immediate dismiss her as an option. But, Nicolette seemed very relieved to have help around the house and not have to concern herself with its general upkeep, which left ample time for her to focus on spending his money. While Lissette appeared to be satisfied that her duties under Nicolette's watchful eye would not be so encompassing that she wouldn't have the energy to complete her evening job responsibilities.

Lissette had been working in the McGillicuddy household for about a month when Patrick came to her while she prepared his and Nicolette's lunch. He told her that it was very close to the time Nicolette should be giving birth and he wanted to pay her double the very generous 75.00 a week he currently paid her to work if she would work for them full time to care for Nicolette and his child once she had given birth. Patrick was well aware of the always urgent need for money in the Baptiste household, that Lissette only made 125.00 a week working both her jobs and, that 150.00 in addition to only working 10 hours a day instead of 15 hours a day would open time for his seduction of her.

Instead of being elated, Lissette was torn. The Fuse family had been very good to her and although not very giving monetarily, they gave her the second hand clothing of their children and any leftovers at the end of her shift to take home to her family. Still less working hours a week and the extra 25.00 would allow her more time to tend to her three daughters and her own household. When she told him she would have to consult with her husband before she could answer, placing emphasis on the word *husband* while completing her statement, then dropping her eyes to the floor.

Patrick reached out and stroked Lissette's cheek before cupping her chin and in his hand, lifting her face from focusing on the floor before her until his eyes were all she could gaze into.

"Madam of course, any respectable man would know that as the case. Please don't take too long with your reply and please, always allow me the pleasure of looking into your eyes as we speak". As if on cue in a romance movie, Patrick released her face, grasped her hand kissed the back of it before exiting the room; as Lissette turned to watch him walk away.

Unbeknownst to the both of them Nicolette stood outside on the veranda watching the entire scene unfold. She knew eventually her incantations and incense would cease to work on Patrick. Now she needed to see how she could work the looming love affair into her plan of domination without losing Patrick's financial support.

With her husband John's blessing,
Lissette agree to work for Patrick and Nicolette
full time as long as Patrick continued to
transport her to and from work. This way she
could arrive home just as the girls were getting
in from school and have dinner with her own
family. But, as the birth of Nicolette's child
grew closer, she grew more demanding of
Lissette's time and work days once again
proved long and tedious. With Lissette
sometimes getting home long after John had
put the girls to bed and left for his nightly
adventure of booze, gambling and random
whores. Usually not returning until after
Lissette had once again departed for work the
next morning.

Meanwhile, Patrick continued what he
believed to be a seduction of Lissette. He took
the long routes in the evenings while
attempting to woo her with stories of growing
up poor and struggling in Ireland, moving to
America and opening his own pub.
Occasionally he would give her small tokens of
his affection.

Lissette had begun to enjoy the
entertaining stories, pastries and small gifts of
jewelry Patrick had begun to deluge her with.
Her relationship with her husband had
deteriorated to the point where they were no

long even speaking and only engaged in sexual contact if he returned home before she left for work, drunk, sweaty and reeking of funky perfume. His touch was rough, unsolicited and loathed by Lissette. Still she felt bound by her religion to him and wouldn't dare speak of divorce.

One evening after a long humorous tale of his youthful mischief by Patrick, Lissette found herself totally amused and dizzy with laughter. Patrick felt her gradual comfort with his presence growing and thought this was the perfect opportunity to make his desire for her known. He stopped the car on the side of the road, lead over and kissed her firmly on the lips. To his surprise and pleasure, Lissette did not pull back but, returned his kiss with the same lust yet the innocence of a virgin.

Lissette surprised herself with the fever in which she returned Patrick's kiss. Her femininity was malnourished by her husband's neglect and, Patrick's passion was welcomed by her spirit, she couldn't stop his advance. As Patrick's hands roamed her body through her thick maid's uniform and touches her soul, removing all inhibitions until the image of her Catholic wedding to John flashed in her mind.

"Stop", she whispered, "my husband Sir." Patrick pulled away.

Mamie's Mayhem by
The1Essence

"Leave him", he commanded her, "I can provide for you and the girls, you know this." Lissette regained her composure and sat erect in her seat.

"No Sir, I cannot. My religion will not allow for it and I will be cast out o'my community as a harlot. My daughters will be shamed."

"Then just move away. I can still provide for you. Everyone knows he is unfaithful and disrespectful to you", Patrick pleaded.

The thought of being provided for and loved by a man again sent shivers through Lissette and she began to cry.

"And, Ma' dam Nicolette and, your unborn child, what about them", Lissette questioned through her sobs.

Patrick pulled back fully in the driver's seat of the old Buick, sighed and pulled the car off the side of the road. She was right but, he would figure out a way to have her for himself. They drove the rest of the way to the Baptiste home in silence with the both of them still wanting the passion burning between them unleashed.

The daily goings on at the carriage house took a more light hearted appearance after Patrick's and Lissette's first kiss. Lissette began to delight in her commute with Patrick and the stolen kisses throughout the day as his visits to check on Nicolette and the baby became more frequent. Patrick didn't even mind the early rise and commute by ferry from the Garden District to the West Bank then back again in the evening. Nor did he believe Nicolette noticed his delight in Lissette.

Even though her Bayou constituents who were maids in New Orleans, or knew maids in the city told her that occasionally Lissette and Patrick were spotted entering or exiting his home some evenings, Nicolette thought she was wrong about her employee's interest in her husband and that his desire for her was returning with his more frequent visits to their home in the country. That is, until she spotted them engaged in passionate embrace in the back yard when Lissette was supposed to be doing laundry. Not one to shy away from confrontation, Nicolette reproached her husband.

"You are mak'ng me loo' like 'da fool with your goings on wi' dis' girl", she said to him as he approached the back door to enter the house. Patrick appeared unfazed by her conviction.

"Who are you to question my actions or hers? As I recall you were in her position not so long ago and had no complaints", he told her.

"It's not 'rite. Her skin may be fair but she is still not a White woman and I know you don't love her. It's her wo'manhood you seek and no'ting more"! Nicolette's blood began to boil at Patrick's indifference. "I want her gone!" She demanded.

Patrick stopped walking toward the front door and turned towards Nicolette's imposing figure still standing in the back doorway, blocking the sunlight.

"Well, it's not your house, nor your money that pays for her service is it? Therefore, it's not your choice. But, you can always leave my child and my home and, return to the husband and child you left behind, that is your only choice. Now, I have had enough of this conversation. I have to get back to the pub. I will return later to take Lissette home", and he walked out the door without further conversation.

The discomfort of pre-labor sent waves of pain around Nicolette's midsection as she realized her plan to create the perfect dynasty here in America was beginning to fall apart. She could hardly blame Patrick for his manly lust and stupidity. But the whorish Lissette was an entirely different matter of contempt; she would be dealt with accordingly at later time. Now was time to focus on the birth of her second child who she knew would sit at her side as Prince of the dynasty she would not let be derailed, even if protecting it meant someone else had to die.

The rest of Lissette's day after Patrick left was long and tedious. Nicolette took to her bed in preparation to deliver her child and her temperament was that of an Asian dictator. She insisted the floors be scalded, windows washed and every article of clothing washed while being relentless in her requests for glasses of ice or ice cold water. By the time Patrick returned, Lissette was completely exhausted.

When he entered the house Patrick was met by the overwhelming smell of bleach and a sullen Lissette who informed him of Nicolette's beginning stages of labor. Patrick became excited at the thought of finally becoming a father, even if the child was a Negro. But, more so about the idea he had to finally make love to Lissette.

"My Dear," he began speaking to Lissette, "do you have anyone you can contact to watch your girls tonight, I have a feeling I will need your assistance here with urgency."

"Oui Misère, my neighbor, Mrs. Watson will look in on them once my husband leaves, until I arrive home", Lissette responded. The thought of spending the entire night with Patrick thrilled her and her face flushed.

Patrick went to the bedroom he shared with Nicolette on that fated honeymoon not so long ago and stared at her from the door. The large, encompassing figure lying in the center of the bed emitting soft moans was nothing like the enchantress he had spent days in that very bed with only a few short months ago. And, she was certainly not a woman to lose his sanity over. Everyday Patrick believed the rumors that she had him under some sort of spell more and more.

"I don' wan' ya here. Your neg'tive energy is bad fo' my chile, go stare at your slut", Nicolette moaned from beneath a pile of blankets.

"Once my child is born you can find your way back to the sharecropper you came from", Patrick spat at her as he walked away.

He joined Lissette in the kitchen where they sat side by side enjoying a meal of jambalaya and corn bread, followed by a bowl of warm peach cobbler and coffee, all prepared by Lissette. After their intimate meal they both tried to entice Nicolette to eat but she would not respond to their pleading.

"Call the midwife at first light!" were the only words she uttered to them.

Immediately Patrick set into motion this plans for spending this entire night in bed with Lissette. He grabbed her hand and led her outside to the swing on the veranda, pulling him onto his lap as he sat down. Her neck smelled of a mild mixture of the Evening of Paris perfume he had recently given her and bleach and, the combination of the perfume, cleaning supplies and the sweat of her skin enchanted him. He began planting soft, sensual kisses on her face and neck.

Lissette allowed her mind to be enveloped by the passionate tenderness she so lacked in her lifeless marriage to John. She lost all fear of being labeled a jezebel in Patrick's gentle touch and, when his fingertips caressed her erect nipples any thoughts of reprisal by disappeared in the haze of lustful whimpers escaping her throat.

They had been intimate before at his home in New Orleans but this time would be different. Patrick did not have to sneak her in the servant's entrance under the shadows of darkness. Their lovemaking tonight would not be rushed and they would not partially dressed.

Suddenly aware of the growing loudness of Lissette's moans, Patrick stood, cradling her petite frame in his arms and carrying her to the guest bedroom she had prepared earlier for this moment where, they both quickly undressed. Not wanting to waste another moment away from the soft embrace of each other's arms.

Lissette slid under the tops sheet of the bed to cover her nakedness but, Patrick slowly pulled them back, exposing the dark brown erect nipples protruding from her ivory body. She so reminded him of his deceased wife, so slight and incredibly tantalizing. Patrick fell into the queen sized with pillow topped mattress beside Lissette. It's softness engulfing them both.

Sounds of intense lovemaking awoke Nicolette from a dark haze she meditated in to escape the pain of childbirth. She couldn't believe Patrick would stoop so low as to bed his new lover in the room next to the one she was about to give birth in. Somehow she found the strength to rise from the bed. Grabbing her tattered book of spells she intended to summon Ogoun with all her might to snatch the lives of the fornicators this very night before her Prince could bear witness to their sordidness. The lovers were so involved they neglected to close the door to the guest room and Nicolette briefly stopped to watch as Patrick made love to Lissette as he once had to her. They didn't hear her stumble out of the house into the encompassing darkness of the bayou. As she clumsily staggered through the Spanish moss hanging from the dense woods the owls began to screech and bats fluttered about her head.

Finding a small fishing boat tied to the edge of a small bank Nicolette got in and rowed until she hit an embankment in the middle of the bayou. Pain racked her body still, she managed to light a small candle and begin her incantation of death to her betrayers back at the house. With every contraction Nicolette's chants grew louder and she began to slowly slide down until she lay flat on her back on the bottom of the boat and passed out.

It has become bayou folklore that Loa himself delivered Nicodemus McGillicuddy in that fishing boat while crying out towards the heaven that he would be the true redeemer. At the exact moment of his birth a unusual rainstorm moved in and ripped century old oak trees across the county.

Nicolette awoke to a profound smell of blood, feces and a bloody baby boy screaming half out of her womb. She held on to the side of the feeble fishing boat with one, lifting one leg to rest on the wooden seat of the boat. Reaching between her legs with her free hand she grabbed the child by the neck, pushed down on her diaphragm and released the child from entrapment with a blood curdling scream that disappeared into the abyss of the bayou.

The stench was almost unbearable for Nicolette. And, she knew that it wouldn't be long before wild animals hiding in the shadows picked up the scent, especially the gators. She picked up a roll of fishing line lying next to her and used it to cut the baby's umbilical cord allowing her to bring Nicodemus to her breast to sup as she rowed back to shore. She didn't dare wash him in the murky water which meant she had to find her way back to the cottage quickly. The death of this child would not only conclude her stay in the lap of luxury but the end of her dream of a perfectly bred family of supreme dominators.

The beginnings of daylight awake Patrick from a blissful slumber, still hold the peaceful looking Lissette in his arms. Startled by the sound of a child crying in the room next to him he quietly shook his lover awake and order her to quickly dress. Together the clamored into the adjoining room where the found a barely recognizable Nicolette breast feeding an angry pale newborn child. She reeked of feces, her usually neat long mane of hair was clumped together in a muddy mess and her entire body was covered in filth save a few exposed scratches on her face and the breast the child was now feeding from. Nicolette greeted them both with an abnormally large smile.

"Meet Nicodemus", she yelled at the top of her lungs at them then she let out an eerie, mind numbing laugh. Patrick and Lissette bumped into one another trying to remove themselves from the gaze of the still laughing mad woman.

The immediate days following the birth of little Nick were filled with silent confusion. Nicolette let both Patrick and Lissette know she was aware of their infidelity and that unless they wanted there impure lives to be further rocked by scandal they would resume life as normal as possible and that she, Nicolette would not be living her home or her son anytime soon. The seemingly doomed couple thought that Nicolette had gone completely mad and Patrick plotted to have her committed. When Lissette learned of his plans she refused to participate.

"You have already doomed my soul to reside in within the gates of hell but, I will not take part in separating that child from his mother", she told him.

Lissette continued working for Nicolette during the day cooking, cleaning and tending to young Nick and, stealing moments of passion with Patrick at night. Shortly after the child's first birthday she found that she herself was with child. Her husband John knew the child was not his but conceived by his wife with Patrick and he began visiting McGillicuddy's Pub to taunt its White owner and solicit a bribe for his silence. He also started beating Lissette ferociously when he returned home from drinking. He cursed her, called her a whore in front of the older girls and spat in her face.

Patrick's friends in town got word of the Haitian immigrant's taunts and banded together one evening to help their comrade rid himself of the nuisance.

"Hang the spook", one of Patrick's friends suggested during the secret meeting after the pub closed.

"No", Patrick responded, "That would be too obvious. And, even though I would never see the inside of a jail, the stigma would still surround me and I risk my business to ruin." Then Neal Jennings, a retired constable spoke up.

"I know what to do. Drunkards are found dead on the ferry all the time. No one would suspect a thing", he volunteered.

"How much will it cost me to be rid of this problem", Patrick asked.

"Consider it a gift. But, you need to shed this obsession with the coon women. Light skinned or not slavery is abolished so, it's no longer acceptable to breed with them."

Patrick shook his head yes and, the plot to murder John Baptiste was confirmed with a round of Jack Daniels for everyone.

Six months later after a horrible beating delivered to Lissette by John, she went into premature labor and gave birth to Jahmiah Millicent Baptiste. The child immediately commanded the attention of her sisters and mother. Pauline, her eldest sister gave her the nick name "Little Momma" because of it, which was Jahmiah later shortened to "Mamie" when she got older.

For almost six months, John vulgarly boasted amongst his friends and at McGillicuddy's Pub about his sexual prowess despite his drinking and how fair skinned the child was.

Incensed by John's bragging and having to give him $1200 in cash and free drinks at the pub indefinitely for his silence, Patrick contacted Neal to set their plot in motion.

One month after John Baptiste was murdered, Patrick was on his way to retrieve Lissette and take her home after a long day of tending to Nicolette and Nick's demands when the brakes on his new Lincoln Town Car gave out as he was maneuvering a sharp curve. The car went over an embankment into a portion of Lake Pontchartrain and, dead, bloated body was pulled from the lake the next morning. The authorities never found out who cut his brake line…And Nicolette's vengeance was only beginning.

Today

Mamie's Mayhem by
The1Essence

Mamie could not stop thinking of the tall handsome man she'd met on Bourbon Street. There was something about him that captivated her. Although she had a feeling that he wasn't very much older than her, there was an even stronger, almost overwhelming feeling that there was a bond between them even though their encounter was brief but, she couldn't put a finger on the bond. Was he her soul mate?

Officer Benton wondered if he should now make his feelings for Mamie known to Lissette. He knew telling Mamie would fall on deaf ears. She was still yet and didn't know what was best for her and, he could protect her from her demons. She was scarred beyond the help of a therapist. Yes, he thought, only he could protect her from herself and, to do that he must make an appeal to her mother. Certainly Lissette would be swayed by the fact that he could provide for Mamie financially and that his job would assure a certain status among their family with security. Mamie was a burden to the old woman financially and mentally. Indeed his offer of proposal would be welcomed as he could support them both.

When Mamie and Officer Thad disembarked the ferry he placed her on his horse in front of him, wrapping his arms around her to hold the reigns steady and

Mamie's Mayhem by
The1Essence

warming her with his body as darkness surrounded them, bringing with it an almost artic chill. Surprisingly, Mamie did not resist him as he pulled her closer and pressed his chest tightly against her back.

For Mamie, there was a comfort in Officer Benton's embrace. She closed her eyes and leaned back, tilting her head slightly so that it rested under his chin. She thought about how often he had come to her rescue and, briefly she thought of the fateful night he came across her after those fiends had attacked her in the alley, taking sunlight with them as they fled. Most of that unforgettable night was a blur to her. In fact, she wished she could dismiss it all of it as a nightmare because since then an uncontrollable darkness had taken over her spirit.

The happy, carefree aura that had once been a personality all around her looked forward to and welcomed was replaced by anger and a menacing, homicidal presence that was destined to bring her to a horrible end. Still she couldn't shake it; or the feeling that Jeremiah McGillicuddy would be vital part of her future. Mamie let her thoughts meld with the warmth of Officer Benton's chest as they continued toward her home.

Lissette listened closely as Officer Benton made his interest in Mamie know to her and Mamie, whom she was sure, was listening in the kitchen. Although he was surely secure enough financially, stable enough mentally and sincere in his want for a better life for her youngest daughter, this union would never take place as long as she lived. Lissette invited Officer Benton outside on the porch and told him just that.

"My dear Sir", she spoke softly and chose her words deliberately and, carefully, "A union between my child and one of Ma 'dam Nicollette's will never happen during my lifetime."

Thad was surprised by her statement. He knew of the folklore surrounding his mother yet, he had never encountered anyone who so willingly scorned him because of it. Lissette saw the surprise in his facial expression so; she tried to soften the blow of her revelation.

"Young man, there are things not known to you that punish my thoughts regarding this. Just know, if there were any way around this I would welcome you into my family", Lissette closed her eyes shivered at the thought of uniting the Baptiste and McGillicuddy family.

"Please, leave us. And, I think it best you not see my child again, in any capacity. I'm sure there are companions of yours on the police force that will certainly look after her in times of trouble."

Lissette then turned around and entered the house, gingerly shutting the door behind her. As she did so the tattered screen door slammed, stirring a powerful uneasiness in her soul.

As Mamie slid into bed, she wondered what her mother had to say to Officer Benton that was such a secret. She was glad she overheard her mother say that marriage would never happen. But, she would not let her curiosity spoil the dreams of love she knew where waiting for her of her true love…Her heart swelled with thoughts of Nicodemus McGillicuddy and, she quickly fell asleep.

Officer Benton stood stunned and silent as he watched the old lady softly close the door in his face. How could she say no? What reason did she have to place the actions of a mother he barely knew on him? Surely if she knew of her mother and her goings on she also knew he had been raised by his father and not Nicolette McGillicuddy!

Anger boiled in a place he had never felt it. His pulse increased rapidly and he felt as if his brain was beginning to swell as he descended the worn steps and mounted his house. Did he not save and protect Ms. Mamie Baptiste time and time again? Had he not proven himself based on his very actions and not those of a demented, confused mother?

No, this was not the last the Baptiste family would hear from him. And, his mother would help him claim his reward or, be damned to hell trying.

The beautiful young woman staring boldly at Cutty in the middle of the street stayed on Rachel's mind all the way home. It seemed Cutty was as interested in her as she was because he spoke of her in broken French with Ms. Nicolette all the way back to the house they all shared in the country. There was no way she was going to allow this little girl to come into their fold and destroy what she and her twin sister had worked so deviously to build. The smell of Canton, Mississippi was still too fresh on their clothes to be met with defeat now. And only jail time for her perverted crimes awaited for her if they were turned back!

Ruby turned up her lips and nose as if she something smelled bad as Rachel told her of the incredible events of her afternoon and the young girl. Rachel had always been super scary and always worried about simple shit.

Mamie's Mayhem by
The1Essence

The Twins

Mamie's Mayhem by
The1Essence

It w

It as Ruby who devised a plan to get out of Canton when 12 year old Martin told his parents about Rachel touching his "privates" when she babysat him.

It wasn't the first time Rachel had acted out her sordid fantasies on a young child. In fact the youngest had only been three years old when Ruby caught her twin sister in the act of molestation. Reporting her to their parents was never an option. Their mother was too busy working and at church to pay even notice that the father of her twin girls had been molesting them both since the age of 5. Their home life put the "dis" in dysfunction. She and her sister only had each other and it was Ruby's job as the eldest to protect her younger sister, even if they were only five minutes apart.

Running from Canton to New Orleans was the easy part. They tried hookin' without a pimp but found it a john would beat you after fucking you simply because they knew they would not have to pay a price to a pimp. Many mornings Rachel would have to scrounge in trash cans for food and begging shop owners to use the bathroom to wash. Until the day they asked to use the restroom at McGillicuddy's Pub. The bartender told them of an old Haitian woman who lived on the outskirts of the city that took in women in need. They quickly agreed to go. He made a call then served them a hot corned beef sandwiches.

When Ruby saw Cutty walk into the restaurant, something deep insider her stirred. She had never been the one to go crazy over men but this man had arrogance about him that she was immediately attracted to. Men had always gravitated towards Rachel even though they were identical twins. Rachel was a couple of inches shorter than Ruby, thinner and always wore a girlish smile that feigned mystery. While Rachel preferred a stern, lowered brow approach. After the abuse she had endured at the hand of her father no man could be trusted. She was of the opinion that the only thing they wanted was nestled between her thighs and they would pay to have it. Love, affection and intimacy were luxuries she couldn't afford. But, this man said something to her with his piercing stare as he walked towards them. The control in his walk made her warm and moist between her legs.

Cutty took one look at the two women sitting at the bar and he knew why he had been summoned. Their clothes were dirty and hair dishelmed, nothing a little soap and water couldn't take care of and, he was quite satisfied that identical twins would be an asset to his fold. Not that business was bad. The droves of horny tourist looking for exotic sexual encounters never ceased in New Orleans. But, twins were sure to be a big demand.

Cutty shook the hand of the bartender when he approached the bar and exchanged cordialities. He leaned on the bar closest to Rachel, and then he turned to the two women and introduced himself.

"Hello, I'm Cutty and, it looks like you two are in need of my assistance."

Rachel stopped eating and extended her dirty hand to him after wiping it on her filthy jean jumpsuit.

"Hi! I'm Rachel and this is my sister Ruby", she giggled.

Cutty looked at her hand then dead in her eyes and, ignored her greeting. Not removing his glare from Rachel, he spoke to Ruby.

"So, Ruby, are you ready to change your life or will a sandwich and the pub's bathroom do?"

Rachel was immediately embarrassed by his piercing look and diverted her eyes to the floor. Cutty then turned his attention and his eyes to Ruby, awaiting a response. Ruby returned his stare but when she went to speak she found the usual bass in her voice that reflected her confidence had been reduced to a whisper.

"Whaaa, what kind of assistance are you offering", Ruby managed to squeeze out before looking away from his flawless light almond colored face.

Cutty moved to the space separating the barstools of the twins. With his back toward Rachel, blocking any eye contact between the two, he focused his eyes on the insecurity he saw in the woman's face; her lips were actually quivering.

Nicolette had groomed him well the last five years on capitalizing on any weakness he found in a woman. Using that knowledge they now had eight women in their stable working of the debt of their kindness. Despite the occasional chastising none of them wanted to leave and, he was sure these two would be no exception. He had not met a woman yet he could not charm and turn out.

Although there was only a slight difference in their physical size he could already tell the smaller one named Rachel was a pushover. He hoped she could count her money after a trick. But this one he had his eyes on now was definitely not a dumb. Still, she turned from him as if she were weak minded. Cutty was sure she was feigning her reaction. He would have to keep a close eye on her.

"Do you have another option pending", Cutty spat at Ruby and began walking towards the door giving Rachel a glance over his shoulder.

"Girl is you craaazy", Rachel said to Ruby as she scooped up the remains of her sandwich and the crumpled paper bag containing her one last clean pair of underwear and another jean jumpsuit, that had been sitting on the newly waxed, walnut planked floor. Rachel quickly grabbed her half eaten sandwich, paper bag and followed her sister out the door. Outside she heard her sister let out a scream of delight.

"Ooooooo weee! This is sharp, come on Sista!"

Ruby took one look at the gold, four door cutlass supreme, spotless and sparkling in the mid-day sun and, the captivating man sitting in the driver's seat and she immediately knew what the noise was about. Cutty knew by the familiar squeal the deal had been sealed. Now came the hard part, these girls were as green as they came, lessons had to be learned. He hated this part.

Ruby watched Rachel quickly tossed her paper bag in the open back window and jump *into the front seat next to Cutty. She decided against sliding in next to her because it was clear that Rachel had set her sights on making Cutty her man. Ruby swallowed her disappointment by biting down slightly on her bottom lip. Rachel always got the best looking guys and, it made no since to fight with her about this one. Besides, she still had no idea where this man was taking them and she had to watch everything he said and did. Protecting Rachel from herself was no easy job but, there was no one else to do it.*

Cutty let out a deep sigh as he watched the quiet twin ease cautiously into to his freshly detailed leather back seat. Hair thick black hair was neatly parted down the middle and held two French braids that rested at the nape of her neck. He would need to get these girls to the hairdresser quick but, after he got them some clothes and a good shower. Yeah, he thought, they are pretty enough to beat these tricks out of some cash still the way she was back there chewing her lip made him wonder if she wasn't still a virgin. He knew the little excited one sitting next to him wasn't. She was too damn silly to be. His thoughts were interrupted by Rachel loudly exclaiming she was ready to go.

"Let's goooooo mannnnnn! I'm ready to get this party started!" Rachel whined loudly.

Cutty raked a patch of hair that had fallen out of place in front with the fingers on his right and while opening the car door with his right. He got out the car but before he closed the door he made sure Rachel's window on the front passenger side of the car was rolled fully down. The sound of the window lowering was drowned out by Rachel once again voicing a complaint.

"Look", she belted out, "I thought we was going to yo place to party. What the fuck we waitin' for mannnn!"

Cutty gently shut the car door and took his time walking around the front end of the car until he stood directly outside the car next to Rachel. Abruptly he reached into the car, filling his fist with Rachel's long, and single, puffed pony tail in the back of her back of her head. Cutty pulled her hair as hard as he could until he had her neck out of the car window then he rammed her forehead into the top of the window frame as hard as he could twice.

"Shut the fuck up Bitch! I can't stand a bitch who talks to goddamn much", he stated through clenched teeth. Then he released her ponytail. Dazed Rachel slid down into the front seat and slumped back.

Mamie's Mayhem by
The1Essence

Cutty quickly glared in the back seat to see if Ruby was going to react. She sat motionless looking out the window towards the opposite side of the street so he continued. Reaching back in the window, this time he gently stroked Rachel's face.

"If you are going to be my woman, there are a few things you need to know about me. One, you don't run shit", he spoke softly, almost in a whisper but loud enough for Ruby to hear; "You don't tell me to do anything or even imply you may be thinking. You don't think. I think for you. I know what you like, what you want and what you need. I tell you what to think"

"Two, keep your muthafuckin mouth shut unless I've asked you to speak. When I say move, you jump your ass up and run around in circles until I say stop and, when I do, you stop; Johnny on the spot. Never forget what I'm telling you okay? If you do, I will beat your whoring ass down in the middle of the street like the funky dog you are", Cutty released Rachel's face and took a step back from the car.

"Now get your Black ass out the front seat of my car. No hoe's ride in the front seat with me. EVER!" Then he returned start to Ruby who was looking at him expressionless.

Mamie's Mayhem by
The1Essence

"You got that", he said to her.

Ruby shook her head yes slowly then turned to stare once again at nothing on the other side of the street. She couldn't speak. She was sure Cutty was young than the 26 years of she and Rachel. But this young man had a powerful presence and she wanted him, in any and every way he would have her. The feeling of passion was so strong; she thought she had peed on herself when he roughed up Rachel then spoke softly as he stroked her face.

"Alright then", Cutty spoke in a cheerful voice, satisfied that the first of many harsh lessons were being digested. "Let's go shopping; ya'll making me look bad."

Two years had passed since that warm November day they were brought to Madam Nicolette's home from McGillicuddy's Pub. Now, she was listening to her sister tell her of a little girl that had captivated the attention of both Madam Nicolette and Cutty which, threated her efforts to become bottom bitch and, her plan to use Rachel to bond this family to them forever. But, ever observant, she would she what developed from this and act accordingly. Even if that meant this young chick would have to come up missing…

Mamie's Mayhem by
The1Essence

Mamie woke up from a restful sleep to the smell of bacon and hot water cornbread. Lissette only cooked breakfast if she had been up all night. Mamie remembered the hushed voice Lissette has spoken to Officer Benton in last night and wondered what was making her mother worry. Mamie decided to be on her best behavior today. She needed Lissette to forget last night so she could find her prince. If Lissette were still upset about her being brought home yet again by the police late at night there would be extra chores to do and no freedom to roam the streets for at least a week. She quickly washed and dressed; walking the length of their shotgun house to the kitchen nestled in the back.

"Ahhh, my daughter finally joins me", Lissette greeted her. She sounded very cheerful which made Mamie begin to worry about just what her mother was up to.

"Who could sleep with the house smelling so good Ma'man? Have you been up all night", Mamie asked, making small talk to see if Lissette would reveal a motive behind such a good breakfast.

"No, Dear. I may not have slept as soundly as you but, I did sleep", Lissette answered as she placed a warm plate of food in front of the seated girl.

Mamie's Mayhem by
The1Essence

"Jaa-Mamie", Lissette began as she sat down at the table, "What are your plans? You are not a little girl anymore. And, it's obvious you do not wish to continue your education past high school. So what do you plan to do with your life?"

"Ma'man, don't start. Let's just enjoy breakfast. It's a beautiful day! Mardis Gras is over and we have our city back."

"No, child, this is important. I imagine you heard the conversation I had with the officer last night?"

"Yes, and no Ma'man", Mamie began to get frustrated. "But, I am glad you told that old man to get lost. What do I look like getting married at 16, And, especially to a police officer? That was just ridiculous of him to ask!"

"I don't think so much so. He has been sort of your protector for this last year. And he is obviously in love with you. But, for my own reasons, I could not agree. I don't think it such a harsh thought that you settle down and have a family, like your sisters. If not, what else are you going to do with little education, scrub floors like me?"

Mamie's face started to flush and her body temperature rose. She wanted to lash out at her mother but, she knew this was a conversation her mother was taking seriously. There would be no easy way out and an argument would derail her plans for the day.

"I really haven't thought about it Ma'maan. I do want to finish high school but, after that I thought I would travel. I want to leave New Orleans. Maybe even go to Memphis or Chicago even. Whatever I do, I don't want to stay here. As much as the tourist enjoy here, I see it as a prison and I am suffocating".

"Well", Lissette interrupted, "that is a start. At least you have an idea. And I have very happy to hear you want to finish school. Yes, very happy indeed. But, for now, I think you should find a job until you can re-enroll in school in the fall. You've missed quite a bit and I am sure you will do well by starting fresh with the new school term. Do you agree?"

Lissette's easiness startled Mamie. What had gotten into her mother? Sitting out of school an entire semester to work? Whatever the cause for her lenience, Mamie was happy to have it and nodded yes with wide eyes.

"Good, it is settled. You work the remainder of the semester and the summer. I have to get to work now but, there is a newspaper on the porch. Bring it in and search the want ads. No goofing of mind you. I need help with the bill since you will not be marrying anytime soon." Lissette stood away from the table and walked out of the kitchen.

"Oh, and do not leave my kitchen unclean. I will expect your usual chores to be done when I return", she shouted behind her as she left the house.

Mamie was just too excited to get out into the real world. A row house on the West Bank or marriage right out of high school would not do for her. Today was the day she started down the road to the exciting life she always dreamed about and the first move to that life was to find Mr. Destiny. She quickly shower, dressed and ran out the door. Stopping first to grab the dew drenched newspaper off the porch to read on the ferry to New Orleans.

Officer Benton didn't sleep a wink the entire night. He lamented the loss of Mamie in his life. And, not only could he not make her his wife but Lissette, however so politely told him to stay away from Mamie. That would not do for him. He had to have her.

Officer Benton feigned illness in his voice and called work, telling them he was too ill to work his shift. Then with last night's bottle of Jack Daniels still controlling his thoughts, he got in his Buick and headed out into the early morning fog to speak to the only person who could help him, Nicolette McGillicuddy.

On the outskirts of New Orleans, the guest house owned by Nicolette McGillicuddy was restless. Cutty had rented rooms for several of the girls to entertain johns in the city; only he, Ruby, Rachel and his mother remained in the house; it was 5 am and it seemed the only one sleeping was Rachel.

Cutty and been writing in the journal he had been keeping since he was 12 years old when he was interrupted by the telephone ringing. He knew it wasn't anyone from the police department because his mother kept everyone very well paid off to not arrest her girls. So, he stopped writing and slipped into the hall just outside her bedroom door. Nicolette didn't whisper but, after answering with an impatient "McGillicuddy residence", his mother lowered her voice barely loud enough for him to make out more than a few words. But, he did here her tell the call to "come now, we must begin immediately." But, who was coming? Cutty settled on finding out soon enough and returned to his room. He had a very unsettling feeling about this visitor and he wanted to finish recording yesterday's events in his journal so that he could be present and on his guard when "whomever", arrived.

Mamie's Mayhem by
The1Essence

Things couldn't be going any better for Nicolette McGillicuddy, she thought as she quickly dressed to meet her first born son. She had a plan for both Thaddeus and little Ms. Baptiste. From the day she found out that her deceitful former housemaid had given birth to her husband's only daughter, Nicolette knew this child would be part of her dynasty. She had hoped to use Nicodemous and this child to create a perfect heir to all she had accomplished since seducing her second husband and establishing financial independence for herself and her second son. But, her son by her first husband, Thaddeus would have to do.

Thaddeus had been raised well by his father. Physically fit from harvesting sugarcane on his dad's farm and excelling in his studies before graduating college and joining the police force in New Orleans, there was no doubt that the grandchild produced from his union with Patrick's love child would be intelligent. And the girl had her mother's radiant beauty, another plus for their off spring. It would be a girl. Nicolette hand burned incense and chanted all night for this gift from Heaven or Hell; either would do just as long as she received what she wanted. Lissette, with her creamy, smooth skin, perfect lips and long flowing hair could not escape her fate. Both she and her bastard daughter would pay a heavy price for the betrayal endured, just as Patrick had paid with his life, so would they. The daughter would have to wait until she had fulfilled her legacy by giving birth to the granddaughter that would carry Nicolette's name into infamy. Lissette's demise would be much, much sooner.

Nicolette was jerked away from her evil thoughts by the sound of a horn blowing in the front of the carriage house. She grabbed her cane and shawl and, hobbled toward the front door. Although she was still a large bodied woman, the agility of her youth was little more than a memory and, the early morning dew always managed to remind her that age was settling into her bones and joints.

Cutty stood just outside the dimly lit extravagantly furnished sitting room and watched his mother flag her unknown visitor to come inside. He was totally caught off guard when he saw his upstanding police officer, older brother enter the house and walk follow his mother to sit on the solid white Victorian loveseat beside her. "What could he possibly want", he thought as she saw the two embrace. Whatever it was, by the look in Thaddeus eyes it couldn't be anything good.

Mamie's Mayhem by
The1Essence

Cutty knew that Thaddeus often helped his mother's whores out of tight situations, never accepting money or gifts in return. But, never before had the come to this house, refusing and, to openly acknowledge them as family. Eves dropping was never Cutty style. His mother always kept him informed of any schemes or treachery she had going on and, the whores were too afraid of the wrath of the McGillicuddy's to hide anything. Something deep inside him told him that this was one conversation worth breaking character for. But, nothing could have prepared him for hearing his mother and his brother discuss the murder of his one-time nanny. But why?

The more he listened he found their plans had to do with Thaddeus's spurned proposal of the young lady he had met on Bourbon street the prior afternoon. Suddenly, he felt a strong desire to protect this woman, and her mother, he had to find her. His eavesdropping ended when he heard the door to Rachel and Ruby's room opening. Quietly he eased his way in the direction of his room. He would question his mother later.

Inside the kitchen, on the far side of the sitting room, opposite the door Cutty listened intently beside, Ruby stood, also bewildered and totally enthralled by what she overheard.

She and her sister's security in this household may not be threatened at all and, she felt herself becoming moist between her legs at the thought of Madam Nicolette and Officer Benton slaying a woman in cold blood.

The three weeks that followed the strange meeting between Nicolette and Thaddeus were uneventful for both Mamie and Cutty. Mamie was had not yet found employment but the relationship with her mother had become closer. They shared smiles and laughs while they cooked together and once, after a rather hearty dinned prepared by Mamie, Lissette even joined her in a brief dance to the radio.

Cutty had begun to worry more at the thought of not finding Mamie and warning her before it was too late. His brother had not returned to the house but several times Cutty had his sleep disturbed by the telephone ringing before sunrise and his mother's hushed conversation that followed. The worrying had evolved into insomnia that made him react to the whores harshly for any small infraction.

They all were on edge and spent as more time on the street making money, which immensely please Nicolette. All but Ruby that is. She had proven more an asset around the house preparing meals and cleaning than turning tricks. She was too cold and uninviting to the tricks. Although she was beautiful and, she and her sister together we at first believed by the men to be a hot ticket to paradise, Ruby would not actively participate, was called a prude, and it was left to Rachel alone to fulfill the fantasies while Ruby collected the money afterwards.

After numerous complaints from customer and just as many beatings by Cutty, Nicolette thought it best to keep her at home as a domestic out of concern of losing the money made by Rachel if they were to dismiss Ruby. For surely the dimwitted Rachel would not stay willingly without her sister and, Madam Nicolette never made any of her girls stay against their will.

Finally on a cold, dreary, wet day Cutty spotted Mamie leaving Café Du Monde. She had stopped to pin her long dark hair into a bun. Even though the sun was not shining, Cutty took noticed of how the blond highlights in her hair highlight her light brown eyes. There was something about them that appeared haunting even though she smiled when he pulled beside her and asked if she wanted a ride to wherever she was going.

Mamie's heart skipped a beat when she found the stranger offering her a ride home was the man of her dreams. She tried to act cool and compose herself but she was sure he saw her eyes dancing in delight because before she could answer he smiled at her then jumped out of the car and held open the passenger side front door of the car for her to get in. As Cutty slid back into the driver's seat beside her, Mamie silently thanked God for bringing him back to her.

Cutty swung the car around in a U-turn towards the ferry and the skies opened up unleashing a blinding rain. He pulled the car into the nearest parking lot and turned attention to Mamie. Surprisingly he found that not only was did she possess a stunning smile but personality and intelligence to match. They talked for hours about everything from politics to travel.

Neither wanted to spend the rest of their life in New Orleans and even though she didn't approve of his or his mother's profession of choice, she understood the necessity of it. "Somebody is gonna do it so why not you." She stated when he told her he was a pimp. Cutty could see why his brother had become so obsessed with having her as his wife, despite her youth because now he was beginning to feel the same way. When Mamie told him she was searching for a job, Cutty didn't miss a beat offering her one.

Mamie's Mayhem by
The1Essence

"Negro paleeese! You ain't that smooth! Do I act like I want to be a fuckin whore to you?? We have been havin' a nice time and now you go and fuck it up!" She yelled at him.

Cutty let out a laugh at how quickly her temperament changed. The fact that she was so fiery amused and excited him. She was definitely different but he wouldn't let her even think she could check him.

"Bitch please; you are probably still a virgin. I don't have time to break whores in. I am offering you a job keeping books, shopping for the girls and running other errands that we may need someone with a little bit of intelligence to do. A monkey could do the job so you would be perfect." He knew the monkey reference would piss her off further.

"What?" Mamie turned up her lips and lowered her eyebrows at Cutty's response. "Then get that funky whorin' monkey you had on a leash with you the other day to do the shit then!"

"She has a job, you don't," Cutty responded.

Mamie remained silent. She would have to figure out another way to deal with him. They were on two different levels and it had nothing to do with the age difference. Guys her age would have never spoken to her like that.

Mamie's Mayhem by
The1Essence

But, for some reason, she wasn't mad at him. She did need a job; still she refused to give him the satisfaction of accepting his offer. She didn't have to. Before she could tell him to just drop her off at the ferry he said what she wouldn't.

"Then it's settled. I will pick you up at the ferry tomorrow morning at 8 when I pick up the girls. Of course my mother will have to give the final approval but, my word that you will work out well will be good enough for her."

"Do you always have to get your mother's permission to make a decision", Mamie quipped.

"If I do or don't should matter to you. Concern yourself with making some money to accomplish your goals. Not with whom I may or may not answer to. The bottom line is, you answer to me", Cutty told her.

Not another word passed between them as he drove to the ferry. When he left her standing at the gate, he didn't know if she would be there in the morning or not or, if she was he would be taking a chance bringing her home knowing his mother's plans. Keeping her close would be the only way he could protect her and her mother.

Mamie's Mayhem by
The1Essence

Mamie told Lissette about the job offer at dinner that night.

"That is wonderful Dearheart! Where will you be working and who are these people? Bookkeeping is so much better a career than domestic work. I am very proud of you", Lissette exclaimed.

Mamie told her she wasn't sure it would work out so she would spare her the details until she had been there for at least two weeks and, that was enough for Lissette.

Mamie had been working for Cutty for a month running errands and keeping count of how much money each girl brought to Madam Nicolette each afternoon. There were eight girls, all of whom seemed pleasant enough to be around except the twins. Mamie found Ruby extremely sneaky as she was always lurking around corners and listening to everyone's conversations but, she had a hard time controlling the whimsical ideals of her sister Rachel who always pushed Cutty to the edge of killing her with mysterious disappearances.

Madam Nicolette was the strangest of all of them. She watched Mamie's every movement inside the house. And, when Mamie wondered outside the house to enjoy the sunshine on occasional afternoon in the surrounding woods she felt the Madam's eyes still watching her no matter how deep into the woods she went. Cutty was the only one in the house who took the time to have conversations with her.

Usually, he schooled her on how to determine if the girls were lying about how much money they made or what physical changes to pay attention to when they reported their earnings to her.

Once one of the girls, Tracy appeared nervous, scratching her arms and head, talking fast and constantly looking around the room very wide eyed. Not once looking directly at her. When Mamie reported this behavior to Cutty, he had her review the books out loud to him and then promptly left the house. Mamie knew he was upset because the wisp of hair in the front of his head separated from its usual neat place slicked to the back with the rest of his hair and fell into a relaxed gentle curl in the center of his forehead. If Cutty pushed it back and kept engaging her in conversation he was just tired. But, if he let it hang, someone was in trouble and cussing and beating of the perpetrator usually came soon after.

On this particular evening, he stormed out of the cottage to his car and speed away. He returned with Tracy in tow by her long ponytail two hours later.

Cutty dragged Tracy into the den he and Mamie used as an office and pushed her onto the couch.

"Lil' Bit, come here", Cutty yelled, using the pet name he had given Mamie on her first day on the job.

Cutty began ripping Tracey's silk button down shirt off. Buttons were flying all over the room as Tracy tried to fight him off. But she was no match for Cutty's strength. After a few moments of struggle and, a couple of hard slaps to her face, Tracy stopped struggling with him and let him remove her shirt as she sobbed loudly. What Mamie saw on Tracy's upper body made her sick to her stomach but, instead of stepping away from the two of them, she moved in closer to get a better look.

The closer Mamie got to Tracy, the small thin lines all over Tracy's arms and breast turned into small black dots.

"Track marks!" Cutty yelled as he slapped Tracy hard in the face again. "The bitch is on smack, lyin' 'bout her count and trickin' off the money on drugs!"

Cutty continued his barrage of insults on Tracy and added more forceful blows with his fist to her head and abdomen until Madam Nicolette appeared in the doorway with Ruby following behind like a pet poodle and told him to stop.

"Leave her to me", she told him. Then she turned to Ruby. "Wash that funk off her body and her hair then present her to me in the sitting room, properly clothed of course."

Madam left the room and Ruby snatched the partially clothed whore off the couch practically dragging her out of the room without uttering a work. But, before she left she gave Cutty what Mamie thought was a look for approval. He responded by turning his back

Mamie's Mayhem by
The1Essence

to her, walking across the plush red carpet to stare out of the window into the yard.

Once he was sure Ruby was out of earshot he walked over to Mamie and hugged her from behind.

"Sometimes", he whispered in her ear, "I feel like I am losing my mind in this place." Then he brushed his loose hair back and, kissed her on her cheek.

"Get your things Lil' Bit, it's time to go home. You've had your first lesson in addicted whores 101."

Mamie never saw Tracy again but, that hug and slight kissed endeared Cutty in her heart forever and solidified her feeling that he was her soul mate, for she often felt the same way.

This is how the McGillicuddy's house was run daily. The whores had to check in with their cash by 2pm to Mamie then be out on the track by 4pm. None except Rachel and Ruby were allowed to stay in the house anymore because of Madam Nicolette's weakening control over the Parish police. Cutty said it was due to his brother's erratic behavior. Bragging and boasting that his mother was a voodoo priestess and that she would have him propelled through the ranks to the top job soon. It seems, according to Cutty that his half-brother had lost his job pining over a woman he wanted to marry but, she wouldn't have anything more to do with him and, he was slowly losing his mind.

Mamie had yet to meet the brother Cutty spoke of frequently and with distain, in the evening when he drove her home. But, Mamie got the feeling that this brother was driving a wedge between Cutty and his mother that would not be an easy parting with a good outcome.

With every passing day Cutty and Mamie spent more time together talking. It seemed he was schooling her in running a whore house, which amused Mamie. Surely, he didn't think this was something she would do forever? Still, she enjoyed his company and his conversation as she found the boys dropping by her house to visit boring and self-centered.

Cutty also began taking her out on the track on the drive to drop her off at home. He showed her all the hangouts the whores picked up the Johns and how to spot a whore tricking off instead of working. It seemed she was always in training. Intimacy only came in a soft touch of her hand or a quick kiss on her cheek as she was exiting his car at the end of the day. She wondered if he had any romantic interest in her at all. Still, she was falling madly in love with him.

At home Lissette was elated that her wayward child seemed to have found something to calm her spirit. Mamie didn't volunteer too much information about her job and, Lissette didn't pry because she didn't want to risk Mamie returning to the dark, gloomy state of mind she was falling in before taking this job. And, as long as none of Nicolette McGillicuddy's son were lurking in around, Lissette was fine with the way their home life was improving financially and otherwise.

The end of summer was approaching and Mamie knew it would soon be time to talk to Lissette about keeping her job and not returning to high school. She had run the conversation by Cutty once but he just looked at her like she was insane, offering no response. Leaving her to play the scene out in her head over and over again to boost her courage to challenge Lissette's "education first" rule. It was during one of these imaginary conversations when Mamie got the shock of a lifetime.

She was sitting in her small office inside the cottage, twirling her now honey blond highlighted locks between the fingers of one hand while resting her head on the hand of the other with her eyes closed. Mamie was engrossed in an imaginary conversation with her mother when she suddenly became aware of another presence in the room. Thinking Cutty was in the room watching her daydream, she smiled and opened her eyes only to find a disheveled, unshaven officer Benton standing in the doorway glaring at her. She could smell his liquor rotten breath before he even spoke.

"Nothing will keep me from having you", he growled.

Mamie sat frozen with fear in her seat behind her desk. She could believe officer

Benton was standing in front of her, in this house, seemingly threating her. She had almost forgotten the anger and the horror of the events that initially brought their lives crashing together in just the few months of working with Cutty. Although she had never discussed any bit of her rape and rage with Cutty, somehow she knew he understood his presence calmed her hidden rage and, humiliation.

Mamie's fear was temporarily interrupted by the dark presence of Madam Nicolette standing next to Officer Benton.

"My son, I have been waiting for you", Nicolette said softly, "come, let's have dinner and discussion." Then she put her hand on his shoulder and guided him away from the door of the room where Mamie still sat wide eyed and in obvious shock.

When they walked way Mamie let out the air she had been holding deep in her lungs. She had to get out of there right away! But, she couldn't leave without explaining to Cutty the entire sordid story. He deserved to know why she couldn't work there anymore.

When Cutty picked up Mamie from the cottage to drive her home, he immediately knew something was wrong by the sad, solemn expression on her face. His observation was confirmed by Mamie's lack of conversation, which she always had plenty of. He pulled over into the parking lot of a little park just inside the city to talk to her.

"Lil' Bit, what's wrong? And, don't tell me nothing because I know you a little better than that," Then he cupped her clenched fists in his hands and pulled her towards her.

Mamie leaned back, looked into his green eyes and burst into tears. She told him everything from beginning to end about her rape, rage and Officer Benton. When she was done, Cutty wiped her face with the bottom of his silk shirt and pulled her close tightly to rest her head on his chest. He had only one question about the whole story Mamie had just laid on his lap. "Where did Thad take her after the rape?" But, the answer hit him before he could ask the question out loud. "Mother", he thought.

"Look", Cutty said to her, "I know you're thinking you can't work for me anymore but, I don't want you to quit. I am going to correct this whole crazy scene for you, for us. You can put your trust on that. Just take a couple days off and try to relax. Don't go cutting anyone up or jumping off the ferry. Shit ain't that deep. I got this handled, believe that," Then he pushed her away from him and held her head in his hand so that he was looking into her blood red and swollen eyes. He could fall so deep in love with her he thought. She was so beautiful, so alive and she brought him so much peace.

"Do you believe I got you Ms. Mamie?"

Mamie stared back into his eyes. A calm feeling rushed over her body and she breathed a huge sigh of relief. She needed someone to protect her from any and everything she feared and that brought on her unquenchable rage. And, she longed for it to be him.

"Yesssss."

"Good! Let's get you home. I'll call you in a couple of days.

When they arrived at Mamie's house Cutty again told her that she needed to rest her mind and that he would handle everything. The look in her eyes and the faint smile she gave as she exited the car told him that she trusted him and believed he would handle everything.

On the drive home Cutty readied himself for the impending show down with his brother and maybe, his mother…

Back at the cottage, Nicolette unveiled her plot to create the perfect heir to her voodoo throne, carry on the family name and, help her elder son acquire the love of his dreams. The older of her two boys by different fathers listened as intently as a drunken man can to what she said. His only concern was holding Mamie and getting his life back together. Anything his mother wanted after he achieved that she would have to get alone.

"Only one person stands in the way of us living the American dream happily ever after", Nicolette spit out as she frowned her face as if smelling something foul. "The girl's mother has to be removed from our path to glory!" Suddenly she had her son's attention.

"How do we do that?" He asked her.

"On the next day that the young girl is here, I will concoct a reason to keep her here overnight and, with the help of my potions, by the next morning our obstacle will be removed." Nicolette, now aware that she and her son are being watched and listened to, lowered her voice a barely audible whisper.

Ruby, who and been sitting outside the kitchen on the swing in the back veranda strained her ears hard to hear Madam Nicolette's plan. She could only make out bits and pieces of the conversation but nothing that could coherently be pieced together.

Weeks ago when Ruby first started hearing of Madam's plan to create the perfect off spring by having Cutty impregnate Mamie, she thought she could use the information to gain Cutty's trust. But, never seeing any signs of affection or even sexual interest on Cutty's behalf towards his little protégée, Ruby dismissed that idea. Now, she had something to tell. Clearly, Nicolette had also noticed no interest in the girl by her younger son, and now had to modify her plans, placing the breeding responsibility on her older child. But, should she tell Cutty, or assist in the plot somehow; hopefully in the end, eliminating the threat Mamie posed to her and her twin sister's security with Cutty forever?

After Thad left, Nicolette went to her room and began her ritual of chanting and lighting incense. Although she was still both respected and feared among those who did, she herself had long since abandoned her practice of voodoo and instead had begun to embrace the spirituality she found in Catholicism. But, she took from it only what she needed to achieve her obscure goals.

Tonight her thoughts were focused on the ultimate revenge enacted on her husband's mistress. Once all was said and done, it was Nicolette who would have the last laugh. Didn't she plot and plan her husband's untimely accident? No one suspected she was more than a grieving widow. Only, Patrick was no fool. He had willed everything thing to Nicodemus.

The house, the restaurant, any money and property belonged to her son. She was again as she was when she arrived from Haiti, poor. But, as long as Nicodemus believe she needed him to be the man in her life, she controlled it all regardless of namesake.

But now, not only would she have her revenge on her husband's lover, she would endear and enslave their child for the rest of either of their lives. Ideally a child between Mamie and Nicodemus would have been the

Mamie's Mayhem by
The1Essence

ultimate air to carry her name into infamy but her younger son showed no interest in his sister. Instead he chose to lie with Rachel, a complete idiot and a natural born whore. Nicolette even sensed a deviant behavior in the whore but, had no proof of it. Nicolette shook her head at the thought a whore commanding her throne.

"Never will I allow that!" Nicolette thought as she slid her massive body into her king sized bed. "Even from my grave, I could not allow that to happen." Then thoughts of the glory in vengeance to come returned and she fell into a deep satisfying sleep.

Cutty's steps were heavy as he walked to his room after dropping Mamie home. He had to figure out how to approach Nicolette without arousing her anger. Once she knew that he suspecting something going on with she and Thad, there was no telling what she would do. But, he knew that his days in Louisiana were coming to an end no matter the end to what was to come in the next few days. And, he welcomed the thought of leaving.

Just as he turned on the light he became aware that someone was behind him. He knew it wasn't his mother. She would have announced her presence. And, it couldn't be Rachel because she was too silly to creep. He turned and came face to face with the sly, unwanted existence that belonged to Ruby.

"What the hell do you want", he demanded.

"I, Daddie, I have something to tell you that I think you should know", she replied.

"Well?" Cutty irritatingly commanded. He walked over to his large oak desk and sat down, throwing his feet over it to rest on top and leaning back in the chair.

He stared at Ruby with disgust the entire time she spoke of what she had overheard his mother and brother talking about. His look wasn't so much directed at her but what he was saying to him. Still he could never let her know that if he wanted to maintain control over Ruby and her half-witted sister. They now had become part of his plan to escape Louisiana, his mother and save Mamie and her mother.

"What makes you think I care about anything you have told me? AND, what did you think you would gain by telling me this", he asked her after she finished revealing her eavesdropping information.

"I jusssst thought you should know that's all. Since the girl works for you and all and you seem like you like her."

Cutty jumped up from his seat and grabbed Ruby by the throat, forcing her body against the wall but not hard or loud enough to wake his light sleeping mother.

"Get the fuck out of here, now! And if you ever concern yourself with what you think I like or how I like it I will snap your fuckin' neck! I think for you! Do I make myself clear! Get the fuck outta here!"

When her pimp set her free of his homicidal grip, Ruby slowly backed away from him and out of the room, not once taking her eyes off his. He looked as though he could really kill her at that moment and she wanted to savor every tantalizing moment.

When he heard the door to her room close, Cutty smoothed the lock of hair that had fallen out of place to the back, to join the rest of his manicured mane. He had to think fast to get Mamie and her mother out of harm's way!

Cutty sat back down at his desk to call a friend he had made in Florida on one of his many trips to pick up girls gone astray trying to make it to the big city. Seeing his journal resting in plain view on the desk, he wondered how he had forgotten to put it away after he made his last entry the night before and if that sneaky Ruby and invaded his privacy. He tossed it into a desk drawer, dismissing Ruby. She knew he if he found out she would certainly be beaten.

Grabbing the receiver off its hook, he dialed a number from memory and a time weary voice answered the phone.

"Hellooo, who dialin' Reetha up this time of night? This betta be wurf it", a female admonished.

"Hey Aretha, this is Cutty", he answered, "I'ma be coming your way with a couple girls in a few days, and yeah, I'ma make it worth your trouble."

"Trouble? Awww shhhit, I got a fix for trouble so make it right Baaaby 'cause Reetha pockets tight."

Mamie's Mayhem by
The1Essence

The next morning Mamie told her mother that neither one of them were going to work because she had the next three days off with pay. It took a little convincing but Lissette called in to work so she could spend the day with her youngest child.

It was a picture perfect day on the West Bank of New Orleans. It seems as if everyone in the neighborhood had the same thoughts and had decided to stay home from work. The sky was the bluest of blue with a few scattered airy clouds, children ran and screamed out loud as they played and the smell of charcoal grills burning littered the air. Although the humidity told of a storm soon to come, it was of no concern to Mamie and Lissette as they laughed and talked to neighbors on their way to take the ferry to town.

Their day was filled with laughter and smiles between them. Lissette looked at her youngest child and for the first time she could remember, she saw that her daughter had transformed in to a woman. It had only been a few months since Mamie had begun her accounting job but, there had definitely been a dramatic change in her daughter and, Lissette was very proud.

Mamie's Mayhem by
The1Essence

Later that evening, after Lissette and Mamie had enjoyed a hearty meal they prepared together, Mamie suggested they take in the sunset on the porch of their aged row house. Lissette settled in her old rocking chair and sighed. She wanted to know more about Mamie's job but didn't want to spoil the mood. Still, something inside her told her that now was the time.

"Mamie, you have changed a lot since you started working and, I am so very proud of this change. Your smile each day has given me hope for your future", she started in her broken English.

"Tell your old mother about your new job. I don't believe you have even told me who you are working for.

The tenderness in her mother's voice startled Mamie. She knew what her mother said was right. She had changed. Mamie was sure Cutty was the key factor in this equation. Her nightmares and anger had all but disappeared and certainly the relationship between her and her mother had improved and now she felt it she was comfortable enough to let the past go and just talk to Lissette.

"Ma'maan, I am happy. I feel free and, I have met a man. We work together, very closely in fact. And, now I pray daily I can be the woman he would want to spend a lifetime with."

Lissette sighed, she had a feeling Mamie's change in temperament had something to do with a young man and, considering her previous disposition that was not altogether a bad thing. But when her child went on to say this man was the son of a Madam Nicolette and that she was actually working as accountant for Nicolette McGillicuddy, Lissette's heart almost stopped. But, she held her tongue and let her daughter finish without interruption.

"So now you know all Ma'maan. My life is beautiful now that I am employed and protected by this handsome, amazing man", Mamie poured out her last sentence to her mother breathy and full of happiness.

"These are good feelings to have", Lissette managed to whisper, "I pray for your happiness daily. But, now I must lay the bones to rest. You have given me much more excitement on this day than I have become accustom to."

They both retired to their respective bedrooms. Mamie lay on her bed and dreamed of her future as Cutty's wife, while Lissette fell to her knees and prayed earnestly for the Lord

Mamie's Mayhem by
The1Essence

to deliver her and her child from the danger she knew was at their doorstep.

The next morning Lissette rose early. She again went to her knees and prayed for strength, for during the night, in her restless sleep it came to her that she would have to go back to the cottage of her past that held so many memories for her and, she had to confront Nicolette McGillicuddy. She had to save her child!

Lissette waited impatiently on the porch for the taxi to arrive. She had been careful not to wake Mamie. She didn't want her to get upset and think that her mother was trying to sabotage her happiness and she could never expose her past sins to Mamie.

By the time the taxi arrived the sky had opened up and released a torment of rain but, Lissette would not be detoured. Once they arrived at the cottage outside of New Orleans, she paid the driver extra so that he would wait for her with the promised of an even greater tip once he returned her to West Bank. Lissette did not allow him to drive her up the winding road to the porch of the cottage. She wanted no witnesses to the conversation that was about to take place. So Lissette walked the half mile in driving rain.

By the time she reached the side of the cottage she knew enclosed Nicolette's bedroom the rain had drenched her clothes but, she her daughter's life depended on her completing this mission.

Lissette rapped on the window in front of her until she saw a dim light appear through the curtains, then she head around the house through the waterlogged grass until she came to the side porch outside the kitchen. As soon as she began to ascend the steps the door to the house swung open wildly, hitting the wall it was hinged to inside the kitchen and Nicolette McGillicuddy stepped out on the porch letting the screen door slam repeatedly behind her until stopped.

"What brings the whore of Babbal to my home at this hour", Nicolette confidently chided the soaked and disheveled woman at the base of the stairs.

"Did you not think I would recognize you? You still creep around deceitfully but, it seems my husband is not here to greet you. Creep no further. Stay right where you are. I don't want you scent for foul my home. What do you want?"

"I want you to release my daughter from employment here and stay away from us",

Lissette spat at her. Nicolette let out a sinister laugh and walked closer to the porch banister.

"You have come to command me to leave you and your bastard be? You have come to command me!"

"YES, I have and only God can help you if you don't comply!"

Nicolette slowly descended down the steps until she stood in the rain and wet grass in front of Lissette. Her massive height and weight had doubled at least, Lissette thought. The light slowly illuminating the storm clouds and their lightening made her appear even more imposing.

"I remember you Lissette Baptiste. I remember how I employed you to care for my household and my newborn babe. I remember how you needed a job because your whoring, gambling husband pummeled you and money, leaving you and your children cold and hungry." Nicolette moved closer until Lissette's face was equaled to her enormous breast and all Lissette was sure she could hear Nicolette's faint heart beat under her voice.

"I remember how you seduced my husband and how you turned him against me, leaving me to birth my son alone with him. Begging him to plant his seed inside you and giving birth to his bastard without thought of my child! I remember you Lissette Baptiste and, now you want me to leave you be? I can not. I will not. Not until your filthy scent has been wiped from memory and your child becomes mine. As she should be!"

Lissette found the strength to take a couple of steps back and look into the face of the woman who had just read her sins out loud for the universe to absorb.

"You are insane", Lissette yelled. "Satan has absorbed you but you may not absorb my child into your madness. Nor can you speak on seduction and being a whore." Nicolette put her hands on her hips and laughed.

"Yes, I am queen of seduction and queen of the whores! But, what is mine is mine and you had no right to take it from me. So now, your life and the life of the young girl belong to me. I had your husband killed and I had Patrick's brakes cut. The only sinner left to seek retribution on is you and, the only way to do that is to take your bastard from you and watch the rest of you worthless life evaporate!" Lissette could not believe what she was hearing.

"You ad murder to your list of sins Nicolette but I say for the last time, you will not take my child's life!" Lissette's hand reached inside her oversized crocheted purse and pulled out a small satchel. Again Nicolette laughed at her.

"Foolish woman! You think I want to kill the child? No, no. She will serve a purpose. Her womb will bear an Heir to my throne. She and my son, Patrick's son will fulfill their prophecy or giving me the perfect heir for me. And neither you nor your cheap bag of tricks will stop me from having this!"

Lissette coward back and clenched the bag to her stomach in horror when she heard of Nicolette's demonistic plan.

"I don't have to try to stop you Nicolette. God will stop you and your madness. This much I know!" Lissette ran past Nicolette to the taxi still waiting down the road for her as Nicolette's body shook with laughter.

Inside the house, just outside the kitchen, Ruby stood. Her eyes were wide and she didn't know whether to be happy or afraid of the conversation she had just overheard. But, she knew if Cutty found her on the watching him and listening to the conversation she would be beaten. So, she quietly crept back to her room.

Cutty was horrified and what he had just heard. Initially he was awaken by the screen door slamming had had gotten up to hook it to the frame for the duration of the storm. But, as he approached the door, what he saw and watch he heard left him mortified. Mamie was his sister? He rushed back to his office to write in his diary, leaving his mother still standing the wet rain laughing like a mad woman and barely missing Ruby standing behind him.

Lissette arrived home drenched, emotionally drained and exhausted. She didn't know if her confrontation with Nicolette had served any purpose other than to reopen wounds and, remind her that sins must be repaid. But she didn't know how to do that.

As quietly as she left she went to her room and closed the door. Her load was lightened to see that Mamie was still sleeping. There was no way she could see Lissette's current condition or know of her mornings activities.

Lissette lie on her bed, not bothering to remove her wet clothes. Still clenching the satchel in her left hand she now laid it on her heavy chest and placed both hand over it. She sighed. It seems in the hour it took the taxi to ferry her home she had aged 30 years. She was tired. She closed her eyes and recited Psalms 23 until she fell asleep.

When Mamie awoke she was surprised to see her mother's bedroom door still closed. That usually meant Lissette was sleeping or praying so, she didn't not wake her for breakfast.

Yesterday had been wonderful. Her mother told her she was proud of her and actually seemed happy to hear about her love for Cutty and the job. Well, she didn't complain about it, which was almost as good as Lissette being happy.

After eating breakfast and washing the dishes Mamie decided to take advantage of another day off and take a walk through the neighborhood. She was surprised to find Cutty sitting in her mother's rocking chair as she left.

"Hey you!" She greeted him with a smile.

"Hey yourself", he said as he stood to give her a hug.

"What are you doing here?"

Cutty gave her a very strong but brief hug. The look on his face as he released her worried Mamie.

"Does it really matter", he answered. "I thought you would want to hang out with me on your day off, he lied.

"I couldn't think of anyone better to hang out with, let's go!" Mamie gave a quick thought to Lissette who was sleeping unusually late but dismissed any worry as exhaustion from the prior day's activities.

Cutty drove Mamie through New Orleans and recited his father's family history, taught to him by his mother while showing her the various properties that had been left to him after his father died. After hours of riding in the car and listening to him Mamie told him that she was hungry.

"Well then, why don't we just stop by my place and get something to eat?"

"Ohhh nooo", Mamie quipped, "It's my day off!"

"No silly, the restaurant we just drove by, McGillicuddy's". Mamie laughed.

"Show off!" She teased.

After they had started their meal Mamie looked at Cutty. They had been together all day without having one disagreement. But he hadn't made any kind of romantic gesture toward her and she wondered why. That's when she noticed he hadn't eaten anything and was only moving the food around on his plate. Plus, after talking all day he became suspiciously silent.

"What's on your mind Mr. McGillicuddy", she asked. Startled by the sudden break of silence, Cutty dropped his fork on the plate.

Mamie's Mayhem by
The1Essence

"What are you talking about, I am eating", he answered.

"Well, if that is eating, it's a wonder you haven't starved to death", Mamie laughed. "Seriously, what's going on?"

Cutty looked up from his re-mashed potatoes and stared at the young woman he recently found out was his sister and hoped his sadness didn't show on his face and, cleared his throat.

"Well, I, well I showed you all of this today because I wanted you to know something about me, something other than my mother's house and whores and stuff." Mamie was caught off guard by his nervousness. Cutty saw confusion written across her face so he continued.

"I am also thinking of selling everything and leaving Louisiana. I have always dreamed of living in New York or Chicago and, I think it's time I made my way, my own life. Free from whores, hurricanes and my mother. And, I want you to go with me."

Mamie was completely startled by Cutty's request. She didn't know whether to be elated that he wanted her to go away him or scared.

"umm, uhhhh, Cutty. I don't know what to say. But, I couldn't leave Lissette. She's old, I want to go but, she would be all alone."

"I thought you would say that and, I want her to go with us. She needs a change too. This city has gotten too small for all of us and I just want to shed some light in both of your worlds. And, some freedom in mine."

"I want to go, but I am not sure Ma'aan will. I will talk to her tonight." Cutty stood up and waved to the server to come over. He gave him 20 dollars and reached for Mamie's hand.

"We should get going. I have a lot of arrangements to make and you have to talk to her as soon as possible. I want to leave this weekend and two day should be enough time for you to pack. I am not taking no for an answer. We are leaving this place."

Both were silent on the way home. Cutty's mind was racing with thought of all he needed to do in preparation to leave. He had to go without arousing any suspicion in his mother. She would definitely know of the impending property sales soon through her City contacts.

Mamie was caught in a fever of young love and excitement of dreams coming true. In her mind her man was staking his claim to her and wanted to provide a new, wonderful life

Mamie's Mayhem by
The1Essence

for her but he wanted to take her mother along too. Mamie would convince her to leave with them. She had to!

By the time the ferry reached the West Bank darkness had engulfed the Parrish and there air was thick with unrest. The old row house nestled in the middle of the quite block was completely dark when they pulled up in front of it.

"Ma'aam couldn't still be sleeping." Mamie thought out loud when the car stopped. "It's not like her to forget to leave the porch light on."

"Do you want me to go in with you", Cutty asked.

"No, I'm sure it's nothing. She is probably in her room reading. I will call you in the morning, okay?"

"Okay. Just make sure you are packed and ready by Friday morning." He reached over and grabbed her hand. "Mamie, I'm serious."

"Don't worry we will be ready."

Mamie waved Cutty goodbye after she unlocked the door. As soon as he drove off she entered the darkened house and immediately felt something was wrong. She called out for Lissette but, there was no answer so, she walked to the back of the house where her mother's room was located just across from the kitchen. The door was closed but not locked so Mamie entered, turning on the light as she crossed the threshold. What she saw sent chills up her spine and she let out a blood curdling scream.

Inside her mother's room was Officer Benton and Nicolette McGillicuddy. Lissette was tied to the rocking chair that Mamie had not noticed was missing from the front porch because of the darkness. Nicolette was sitting on the edge of the bed very close to the rocking chair with one gloved hand on Lissette's as if she were saddened by her current plight and Officer Benton was standing behind Lissette with a knife to her neck. Lissette's long salt and pepper hair was disheveled and her face bruised signifying to Mamie that she had been beaten. Mamie tried to compose herself as she felt rage building inside of her.

"Why have you done this to my mother", she asked to neither of them in particular. Nicolette turned to face Mamie without taking her hand off of Lissette's. Officer Benton only stared angrily at Mamie.

"Child", Nicolette began, "its time you learned some things about your precious mother'.

Mamie's Mayhem by
The1Essence

"NO! STOP IT!" Lissette screamed. "You have me. Leave her be! LEAVE HER BE!"

"You are right Mrs. Baptiste. There is no need for any further condemnation as it seems you have indeed accepted your fate. Are you ready now? Have you prayed to your precious Jesus to prepare your place with him"? Nicolette laughed at the thought of Lissette going to Heaven.

Mamie tried to lunge at Officer Benton but Nicolette stepped in the way. Grabbing Mamie by the arms and pulling them hard behind her, Nicolette held her steadily as Officer Benton put down the knife and gaged her with Lissette's head rag. Nicolette continued to hold the struggling Mamie firmly until Officer Benton returned to Lissette and gagged her also.

Lissette's eyes focused firmly on Mamie's. A lone tear slid down her face when Officer Benton raised her chin, exposing her full neck and the age it bore. Mamie broke free of Nicolette's hold on her just as the knife slashed her mother's throat almost severing the head from the body. Blood spurted on the walls and Mamie as she slipped and fell to her mother's feet screaming "Why", over and over again. But, her muffled screams were only heard by uncaring ears until a hard kick to her head by Officer Benton rendered her unconscious.

"My son, let's finish this and each claim our prize", Nicolette hauntingly said to her first born son as she handed him a recently filled hurricane lamp, "I will be waiting in the car." Then she turned and left the house through the back door.

Lust began to build inside of Thad. He would finally get is wife and he had the love and affection of his mother he missed growing up. Killing the woman who kept him at away from Mamie and sent him into the arms of an alcohol addiction that caused him to lose his job was a very small penance to pay.

He grunted as he poured the kerosene from the lamp over Lissette's corpse. Then he picked the still unconscious Mamie up and threw her over his shoulder as easy as picking up a five pound sack of potatoes. Just as he exited the room of doom her stuck a match on the door jam and tossed the flame on to Lissette's body, igniting her clothes and then the room and then the home. The smell of the jasmine perfume Mamie was wearing over shadowed the burning flesh and he wanting male member grew instantly hard.

When he reached the car where his gloating mother was waiting, he tossed Mamie in the trunk just in case she woke up while they were fleeing the scene. Even though his clothes were soaked with Lissette's blood, he cruised through the darkness, past all the screaming neighbors and fire trucks as if going on a Sunday drive, with his elderly mother at his side.

News of the fire and Lissette's murder spread through New Orleans like wild fire. Cutty was making his nightly rounds collecting money from the whores when one of them told him about it and that no one knew where the old woman's youngest daughter was.

He rushed home to find his mother asleep in her favorite chair in the formal living room. He was sure his mother and brother has something to do with the fire and, maybe the murder too. But, if he was going to find Mamie he had to play it cool.

"Mother, mother", he called out to her, "There has been a fire!" Nicolette stirred from her deep sleep and address her son but did not open her eyes.

"Mmmm, I heard. Ruby and Rachel informed me when they arrived earlier. Do not fret over your little panther. She is resilient. I am sure she survived."

"What? Survived? Have you no sympathy or concern for anything?"

"My precious son", Nicolette opened her eyes and stood up. "I am quite aware that you have grown very fond of the child. But, make no mistake on my part. To me she is nothing more than a stray animal you have brought home to train."

Cutty watched his mother walk away from leaving the smell of kerosene and a familiar fragrance that reminded him of Mamie's hair in her wake. He knew she had something to do with the murder of Lissette. If Mamie was indeed alive, he would stop at nothing to find her. And, to do that he knew he would have to find his brother.

Thad headed to his favorite hiding spot, turned into his now home. He had long since sold the land the small was built on. He had inherited the land from his father after his death. For a long time he rented the land to sugar cane farmers around the Parish looking to increase their crop profits for a year or two. But, when he lost his job he was forced to sell the land and live off the profits.

No one knew where the cabin was deep in the bayou outside of New Orleans. He told everyone including his mother that he still maintained a small house in the city. He loathed living in complete isolation and he blamed Lissette for bringing about his decline in what was once upstanding, honorable life.

That was all over now. Lissette was dead and when the sun rose he would begin his life all over again with Mamie. He knew she loved him. He just had to show her how much he loved her. He had killed for her, for them. His mother had prophesized it. They would be happy together.

Thad parked his Sunbird in the low marsh a half mile from the cabin. When dropped Nicolette home he had cooked up a small amount of heroin and injected it into Mamie's arm to keep her lethargic on the ride to the cabin. Now he popped the trunk and saw that Mamie was still knocked out.

He wondered how she would to react to him when she awoke. If she would see that all that he had done that night was for them both. He prayed she would finally return his affections for her. But, just in case, there was more heroin to keep her in check until she did.

Thad smoothly lifted the dirty and bruised Mamie from the trunk and carried her the last half mile to the cabin. He had spent the last week making sure it was clean and presentable for this night, throwing out all the gin bottles that he had been collecting on the floor, mopping and even washing the bed linens.

Once inside he gently washed the still unconscious Mamie, pausing to let his fingers wrapped in the soapy wash cloth linger between her legs momentarily, then moving on just a little faster when he felt his hard on return. He wanted to wait until she was awake to experience their first intimate moments together.

After Thad had Mamie tucked into the freshly made bed he headed back to the bathroom rid himself of the horrible kerosene smell and Lissette's dried blood. Every drop of the shower's steaming hot water began to shed light on his conscience. A few short months ago he was a police officer, sworn to protect and serve. As he scrubbed an innocent woman's blood from his hands and face and, watched it flow down the drain the reality of what he had become began to soak in. He was an alcoholic, ex-cop turned murder, obsessed with a woman seven years younger than him. Now he could add murderer and kidnapper to that list and, the fact that there was a part of him that really didn't care as long as he was with Mamie made him throw up.

While he was standing in front of the bathroom mirror shaving, he heard noises coming from the main part of the one room cabin. Calmly, he set his razor down on the sink and went to investigate. Mamie was awake and had fallen while trying to get out of bed.

"Aww baby, come on. Get back in bed. You've had a long day", he whispered as he walked across the room and reached for her. Mamie's eyes widened as she saw Thad coming towards her and she tried to scoot away from him when he tried to touch her.

"Get, get away from me! Don't touch me! Wh whh, where are my clothes", Mamie screamed. Her head was spinning and her legs felt like lead. She couldn't move any further away from her as her back hit the wall just on the side of the bed.

"Get away from me!" Mamie screamed again as Thad lifted her from the floor.

She tore at his face with her nails, drawing blood as Thad pulled at her waist in attempt to lift her. The sting for the scratches and her efforts to fight him began to anger him. He slapped her hard once, then twice.

"Shut up! Shut the fuck up!"

Thad stopped trying to pick her up and stomped to the other side of the room where a half pint of gin sat waiting for him. He opened the bottled and drained half the contents then stared at the half filled hypodermic needle filled with heroin that lie on the table.

Mamie was still on the floor. Her head was spinning. She struggled to clear her head and think of a way to get out of the cabin but, her body wouldn't move when she commanded herself to get up. Tears began to flow from her eyes down her face as she stared at the man she knew as Officer Benton.

"Oh, you wanna cry? This is NOT the way this was supposed to turn out!" Thad screamed in her direction.

"We were supposed to be MARRIED! YOU were supposed to be my WIFE, have MY babies! But your momma, THAT WHORE said NO!" Mamie glared harder at Thad when he said "whore".

"Yes! Your mother! Mrs. Christianity was a WHORE, and is now burning in whore hell!"

Thad started laughing at the fact that "whore hell" made no sense. But, nothing he had done since having his proposal turned down by Lissette had made sense, he thought to himself.

"It, it didn't matter", Mamie half spat and half whispered. Thad stopped laughing and looked at her.

"What didn't matter", he asked, hoping she was speaking of all he had done. Mamie locked eyes with Thad.

"It didn't matter that my mother wouldn't let me marry you. It didn't matter because I don't love you and I don't want you. I would have never agreed to marry."

The calm in Mamie's voice sent daggers of pain into Thad's heart. Darkness engulfed his mind and anger took control of his body. He rushed toward Mamie and kicked her with his full bare foot in the stomach.

"Ugghhhh"!

The force of the kick pushed all the air out of Mamie's lungs and she struggled to breathe. Thad reeled back and ran away from

Mamie to the wall on the opposite side of the room, watching her naked body heave as she struggled to breathe. He slid down to the floor and began to cry as he sat.

"I'm sorry, I am so sorry baby. I didn't mean to hurt you. I don't want to hurt you. I love you. Just let me love you." He pleaded with Mamie through his tears. But the glare in her eyes as she stared at him through labored breathes told him that was not going to be accomplished easily or willingly. He knew what he had to do.

Thad stood up and once again walked over the small wooden table where the gin and the heroin lay. He downed the remaining contents in the bottle and picked up the needle, staring at it in his hand as he spoke,

"You love me. I know you do", he whispered drunkenly. "You just ain't thinkin' clearly. You ain't thinkin' clearly because you been through a lot tonight. This right here, this is feel good juice. It's gonna help you see that you do love me."

Thad felt a fever rise inside him and stand up in his crotch.

Two months had passed since Lissette Baptiste died in a suspicious fire in her home. Initially the authorities searched frantically for the missing Ja'maiah Baptiste, otherwise known as "Mamie". But once the investigators found heard through neighbors and her sisters that Mamie was very rebellious and longed to move to New York or Chicago they soon gave up the search, believing that she had just run away from home.

Cutty watched the news daily in earnest, hoping to hear even a small amount of news that would lead him to his brother. None of the girls on the strip had seen him and his landlord said he moved out shortly after he lost his job to avoid eviction. Cutty had even visited the farm once owned by Thad's father. Only to find that Thad sold the farm around the same time he'd moved from his apartment. He had even given his telephone number to unsuspecting neighbors near Mamie's West Bank home. Telling them he was a good friend of the family who unlike the police department, would not give up the search for Mamie. They all promised to call him if they heard anything or saw Mamie. Cutty was at a complete loss as to what move to make next. This is until one of the neighbors went to the police and told them they had seen the former Officer Benton driving by the house with an obese elderly woman in his car the night of Lissette's murder.

The neighbor recognized Thad because he had brought Mamie home when the girl had stayed out too late or gotten into some kind of trouble in the city. And, he was often seen sitting outside the home well after the lights were out inside. The detectives immediately launched a massive search for their former counterpart and soon after the evening news broke the story that the case for the missing teenager was reopened, flashing a picture a picture of Thad in uniform. Cutty watched the news break from the bar at McGillicuddy's. Fear instantly encompassed his body at the possibilities what Mamie may be going if she were indeed still alive.

The last two months had been extremely chaotic at the house. Nicolette was not her confident controlling self with him or the girls. Instead, she deferred any questions, comment or quarrels the whores brought to her to Cutty. She referred to herself as Mrs. McGillicuddy, no longer "madam". With Cutty she seemed gentle for the first time in his life. Often stroking his hand or touching him in some way, as often as she could. Even taking time to mention to him often how old she felt and, that her time to enjoy life was winding down. Once, she even asked him would she lay eyes on her very own grandchildren before she took her last breath.

"My son, my precious son, when all have abandoned me you were my constant love. I have loved you the only way I knew how", Nicolette told him one evening after they shared a quiet dinner on the veranda.

But, Cutty wasn't buying her "old woman" act. He despised his mother for taking part in Lissette's murder and Mamie's disappearance. He was sure it was Thaddeus that called her every night after midnight. He could hear her whispering to the person on the line in French but he could not make out what she was saying. The calls were always brief and immediately afterwards Nicolette would light incense and go to bed. The day after the new aired that Thad was their prime suspect and urged anyone with knowledge of his whereabouts to contact the police, the midnight phone calls stopped.

"Stay away from me and my son. Come here and you will regret it", was the only thing Cutty could hear Nicolette's labored voice say just before she hung up the phone. That night neither she nor Cutty slept. Both lie away wrought with worry for very different reasons.

Cutty worried time was running out to find Mamie alive and, Nicolette worried her reign as queen of the McGillicuddy dynasty was coming to an end.

Mamie had no sense of time. She didn't know how long she had been held captive in the small cabin being raped over and over again by the always drunken Thad. She didn't know if it was day time or night because Thad had boarded the lone window in the cabin shut from both sides the morning after she arrived.

Thad was still shooting her up daily with heroin to keep her in control. Initially he tied her limbs to the bed when he went out to keep her from escaping. But gradually, as Mamie regained control of her thoughts she convinced him to leave her unbound by feigning affections toward him. She learned to control her thoughts of escape, and revenge when he was present and savored every moment she was allowed to spend alone in the bathroom bathing. Still, her mind was never far from crafting a scheme of escape.

Mamie began to notice a pattern in Thad's coming and goings. Once a day he left for a lengthy time period and returned with food, drugs and of course, gin. When he returned Mamie would run to him, throw her arms around and pretend to weep and whine of missing her "feel good daddy". Thad fell hard for Mamie's act. But, not hard enough to give her more freedom or even let her go outside.

Mamie's Mayhem by
The1Essence

Then came the day when things took a turn for the worst. Thad came back to the cabin already drunk and in a tirade and yelling that he never should have trusted that evil witch. He paced back and forth in the small cabin, holding his face in his and sobbing. Finally he looked at Mamie sitting on the edge of the bed staring at him.

"We're leaving this place in the morning", he said suddenly calm. Mamie's mind began racing with methods of escape.

"Really daddie? Where are we going? Chicago"? Mamie mustered up a fake smile.

"No, no, Haiti. I have family there. They will help us get settled, I can get a job and we can start our family, like we talked about."

Thad's voice was full of hope and happiness but even in his drunkenness Mamie could tell he was scared. Something had happened and she hoped that it was someone coming to help her. Deep down inside she longed for it to be Cutty.

"Oh, okay daddie", Mamie continued her ruse,
"But, I really would love to go to Chicago, to see snow and"…

"Shut up, SHUT UP"! Thad yelled, beginning to pace back and forth again. "I can't think with you babbling"!

Mamie's Mayhem by
The1Essence

Mamie lowered her head and folded her hands on Thad's checkered flannel shirt she had been using for clothing since her imprisonment. She learned quickly that his drunken tirades ended up with her being beaten followed by him raping her until he passed out.

"I'm sorry babe, I am so sorry", Thad had sat down beside Mamie, put his arms around her and began kissing the side of her face. With every kiss Mamie withheld the urge to throw up.

"Here we are getting ready to start our new life together and we are arguing", he whispered, "let's not fight anymore." All Mamie could do was free the silent tears she tried to hold inside.

"Please", Thad pleaded softly, "don't cry." Then he stood up in front of her grabbing her hands.

"You know what I'm gonna do? I'm gonna run out and get a few supplies, ANNND, I am gonna pick you up a couple of nice outfits for our trip! You'd like that wouldn't you baby? You stop crying then"? Then he walked over to his back pack sitting on the table.

"Yes, daddie", Mamie answered softly without looking at Thad.

"Good but, before I leave", he started toward Mamie with a syringe full of heroin,

Mamie's Mayhem by
The1Essence

"I'm going to have to give you a little "feel good juice", make sure you get enough rest. It's going to be a long trip."

"No daddie, please no", Mamie begged, "I don't need that anymore. I can sleep without it"!

"SHUT THE FUCK UP BITCH!" Thad yelled.

"I know what the fuck you need".

Thad walked up over to Mamie, and with his free hand he balled a fist and struck Mamie in the head over and over again, despite her screams and pleads for him to stop, until she passed out.

When she awoke the cabin was pitch black and it took a while for her to gain her focus. Thad had taken the one lamp in the cabin with him when he left. Mamie stumbled in the direction of the bathroom and turned on the light. When she stood up and stumbled towards the bathroom she felt the no familiar ooze of Thad's semen running down her legs.

"Son of a Bitch", Mamie spat out loud. "You will pay for this shit!"

Looking in the mirror, she saw the affect the drugs and beating had on her face and skin. Her eyes were bloodshot and where ever there wasn't a purple and green bruise her once naturally tanned skin had turned a pasty gray.

Mamie's Mayhem by
The1Essence

Mamie washed the dried blood away from her lips then grabbed Thad's oversized, hooded house robe from its hook on the bathroom wall. When she walked back into the cabin's main room her eyes were focused and she noticed a crack of light along the length of one of the walls. As she slowly walked toward it she realized it was the door! In his drunken haste Thad had forgotten to chain the door from the outside.

Mamie stopped breathing for a moment. What if he was testing her? What if he was standing on the other side of the door? Mamie remembered Thad's razor he used to shave with was on the bathroom sink. She ran back to the bathroom to retrieve it. Her hand shook uncontrollably as she removed the tiny razor blade and headed back towards the door tripping over his muddy galoshes. She quickly pulled them on. She eased the door open just a little bit at a time until she was able to slide out of it.

The night air that filled her nostrils was more intoxicating than the drugs running through her veins. Mamie smelled freedom! But she couldn't move too quickly. She scanned her surroundings and as far as she could see there were only oak trees and weeping willows greeting her. No Thad in sight

Mamie's Mayhem by
The1Essence

so, Mamie leaped off the cabins porch, half running, half stumbling into the night...

Thad was sweating profusely as he left the cabin and raced towards his car. The only thing occupying his thoughts was how he was going to get in and out of the all night department store without being recognized. Earlier in the evening he had called his mother who informed him that there was a massive manhunt for him. Someone had identified him leaving the scene of the murder. It was only a matter of time before the police came to question her. And, she didn't hesitate to say that she wanted nothing else to do with him. It wasn't until he started driving down the dark dirt road that he remembered he had forgotten to chain the cabin's door.

"Shit!" He screamed.

He had only given Mamie half the dose of heroin that he usually gave her. He needed her coherent for their escape. He spun the car around and head back. But he spun so quickly the dirt from the road clouded his vision and he ended up driving into a ditch on the edge of a sugarcane field. He got out the car to inspect the damage. He would have to push the car out but he needed help and, it was a long walk back to the cabin. When Thad rose from the ditch, the headlights from at least four police cars popped on.

"Freeze Thaddeus Benton! You're wanted for the murder of Lissette Baptiste!"

Thad froze in place, wide eyed and sweating profusely. Then he sled backwards down the ditch and ran into the cane field…

Mamie staggered through the wet marshland using the moonlight to guide her. Her head was still spinning from the drugs that Thad had given her and the feeling of freedom but, she couldn't stop, there were too many poisonous predators living in the bayou and, waiting for the opportunity for an easy meal.

By the time she stumbled upon a dimly lit old shanty, she was exhausted and felt as if bugs occupied every orifice of her body. Mamie started down towards the shanty. The gravel on the road felt like marbles under the oversized galoshes. Mamie slipped and fell; hitting her headed on the hard gravel and was knocked unconscious…

Tyrone Turnbull had spent three years fighting in Vietnam. He had seen, learned and done things he could never speak of. No one would understand the things he had to do to survive or the daily nightmares they caused. When a piece of shrapnel almost severed his leg completely off, the Army discharged him with honor and sent him back to the States.

Tyrone had no family to speak of. His wife left him while he was overseas, taking his only daughter with her when she moved to Wisconsin. Instead of seeking them out, he returned to his hometown of Detroit to complete his rehabilitation. Once the Veteran's Hospital discharged him he tried to find work and live in Detroit. But, drugs and violence had begun to take over the city. He had seen too much of both in Vietnam and wanted no parts of it. So, he became a vagabond of sorts. Having his 100% V.A. Disability check sent to his sister's address in Milwaukee, which she took to the check cashing place and wired him the money wherever he may be once a month.

He came upon his current residence quite accidently. It was an old sugarcane farm that was occasionally rented out to neighboring farmers. He actually squatted in an old trapping cabin a few miles away when the owner suddenly turned up. After talking with the man for a few hours and finding him in dire straits, Tyrone offered to buy the entire farm from him with the money he saved while in the military. The owner immediately agreed with one condition, that Tyrone allow him to stay in the cabin occasionally.

While waiting for the deal to close, Tyrone built his little shanty. He chose the spot because it reminded him of the places he would sleep when he was fighting in the war. Even though the trapper's cabin had electricity and running water, the shanty did not and suited Tyrone just fine. The night sounds and simple life suited him verse the horrors and dismay he had experienced in the real world. And he had 20 acres of land to protect him.

When he got lonely for someone to talk to he would get into the rusty old pickup truck he acquired soon after he bought the farm and drive to the nearest Jitney Jungle. There was always someone at the rural grocery store willing to strike up a conversation.

On this particular brilliantly bright morning, Tyrone was headed to Jitney. He had gotten a bit low on supplies plus, there was a cashier that worked there he had grown quite fond of. Today he thought he would muster up the courage to ask her out. His only hope was that she would not say, "No".

Mamie's Mayhem by
The1Essence

That's when he saw the body. The color of the skin told him that whoever it was either dead or almost dead. He hopped out the truck and inspected what he found was a young girl. Her hair was filthy and matted down, her face badly bruised; there insects crawling all over her and the wet house robe she wore. Tyrone felt for a pulse that's when he noticed the track marks on her arm.

"Well, you alive, that's for sure, barely." He said to the girl as he loaded her into the back of his truck.

Cutty was distraught. So many things had happened since that February day when he bumped into a tiny, sassy girl he would come to know as "Mamie". He wrote in his journal every night since then about how infatuated he was with her. His only saving grace is that he had never acted on his enchantment. She was his sister. He had tragically overheard and recorded that information. Now, her mother was dead, she was missing or dead, his mother has something to do with both and his brother was on the run from the authorities for the same. Somehow, he felt, he had to make it all right.

Since the night Thaddeus had escaped from the police, Ruby and Rachel could talk of nothing else. But, they only did so out of earshot of Mrs. McGillicuddy, as she now wanted to be address and Cutty. Both had become very volatile since the police visited the cottage inquiring what they all new of Thad's whereabouts. All stated emphatically that they didn't. But, Ruby did.

She had been screwing Thad since he showed up at the cottage after he lost his job. She overheard him talking to his mother about his infatuation with Mamie and thought she would be able to use him to get rid of her.

That way she could figure out how to get Rachel pregnant with Cutty's child. They needed the security of his money. And, there was no way they were going back to Mississippi. Especially since she'd found out through friends that those little boys her sister molested had growing up, and some of them were now talking about what happened to them at the hands of Rachel's sick mind. She liked them young, that's for sure, and the younger the better.

Only her plan didn't work. Nicolette convinced Thad to murder Lissette and run off with Mamie. And, Cutty was so emotionally unbalanced that she and her sister felt his rather every time he saw them look at him for more than a second or two. Poor Rachel got it worse than she did. She just didn't know when to shut the hell up.

Still, a few weeks after Thad escaped, she intercepted a letter in the mail. Because she had taken over Mamie's responsibilities, no one suspected a thing. The letter was actually addressed to her from a Nathaniel King. When she read the letter she realized it was from Thad. He told her not to worry. He was fine and inquired about Mamie's wellbeing as if he knew she was now with them. He also wrote that he still had plans to come back for Mamie.

Mamie's Mayhem by
The1Essence

The letter, which Ruby burned with the daily trash that evening, had come from Chicago, Illinois; she memorized the address before burning the letter.

Tyrone and Mamie hit it off really well. She had been with him three months and he had helped her kick her heroin habit. That wasn't an easy task. The young, resilient woman had more demons to exercise than the drugs he plight had her body and mind addicted too. This actually made Tyrone more determined to help her. They had something in common.

Initially, Tyrone slept in the cab of his truck to help his houseguest feel comfortable and, to keep watch over her at night. After the first month of Mamie's stay he took to sleeping at the trapper's cabin. He would have rather had her stay there since it had electricity and running water but he knew that would not be an option for Mamie. He knew well of the torcher she had endured there, for many nights he listened to the beatings and rape she suffered in that building.

He had awakened in a terrible sweat one midsummer evening four months ago. Thinking that a walk and a chat with Thad would ease his distress, Tyrone walked over to the cabin to see if his friend was there. The sounds he heard chilled him and enraged him at the same time. His military training kept him from immediately interfering. He had to figure out how not to endanger the life of the woman inside. In order for him to take any actions he would have to release his suppressed urge to kill. It appeared that life back in the United States was beginning to resemble his tour in Vietnam. So, he quietly crept over to the cabin every night after that just to make sure the woman was still alive, regardless of the quality of that life. Finally, his conscience convinced him to drive to Jitney Jungle and make an anonymous call to the police. The next morning he found Mamie on the road outside his home.

Now daily life took on an optimistic journey for the both of him. Mamie shared her tragic story with him. For the first time in her life she had someone she could talk to that she was not afraid would judge murderous thoughts. She felt Tyrone understood her dark side as he would often hear him screaming and crying during the night from outside the shanty.

Tyrone never talked to Mamie about his negative experiences in during the war. He didn't have to. His nightmares told the stories for him. Instead he chose to focus on happier times in his life with his wife and young daughter and the friends he made overseas. When Mamie did ask about his family he told her everyone was dead.

"I was alone in the world until the Lord saw fit to send me a dove disguised as a little girl", he told her. Mamie smiled inside and out.

Tyrone made Mamie feel a love for him like any girl would feel for a doting father. This was something that she had never experienced before, with her own father having passed away when she was very young.

Tyrone in fact took a fatherly role in caring for Mamie, staying up with her all night when during her detox from heroin, spoon feeding her when she was too week to eat, cleaning up the vomit during her darkest times and even driving all the way to Gulfport, Mississippi to buy her clothing and feminine care products. Mamie never went with him on his trips off the farm and Tyrone understood her need to escape the madness of the real world so, he didn't insist. He knew very well that they both would leave their sanctuary to face their demons in their own time.

When Mamie started feeling light headed and throwing up soon after she kicked her forced drug habit, it was Tyrone who told her she had a baby inside of her. That revelation seemed to cause Mamie to withdraw into her own dark nightmares. She became introverted, laughing and smiling and talking less. The only way Tyrone could draw her out was to talk about his life before the war.

One day Mamie asked Tyrone if he had ever killed anyone. He could see the wheels of revenge turning in her head.

"Who do you wanna kill little girl? That man is gone. He can't hurt you no more. And as long as I am alive I won't let him hurt you or that child in your belly." He told her.

"I think", she responded, "I think, time will come when I may have to kill someone. If not him, someone else. And, I wanna be ready."

Tyrone sighed. He knew what she would say next before the words even left her mouth and, he didn't know if he could do it without surrendering to his dark side.

"Teach me what you know please. I need to know how to protect this baby. I need to know how to survive out there because I can't hide forever."

Tyrone set down the fish he had just caught for their dinner on the ground and walked off into the woods. Twenty minutes later he returned carrying an olive green, oblong sack. He walked over to Mamie who was lying on her back in the back of his truck rubbing her stomach and threw the bag in the truck next to her.

Mamie's Mayhem by
The1Essence

"That there is my rucksack. It weighs 75 pounds or more. I carried it with me everywhere in 'Nam. In it, I have everything I need to survive in this world, now you do too." He told her. "Now, I'm going to get cleaned up. You need to get up and clean that fish so we can eat." Then he walked down the road. Mamie watched him until he disappeared.

Mamie had never touch raw fish let alone cleaned one. She sat up and began to dump the contents of the bag in the truck. Inside the back several unloaded guns and loaded clips. There was a camouflage helmet, a small green canteen, wool socks, and a tent with small metal poles and stakes. But what caught her attention were two sheathed knives. One was about 4 inches and the other seven.

Mamie took them both out of there protective covering. The smaller one was completely smooth and looked dull. The larger one was more menacing. It had long serrations that looked like teeth resembling a saw and a small hole in the longest tooth at the end. Mamie grabbed the smaller knife, slid off the truck and headed towards the fish still lying on the ground near the shanty.

Descaling the fish was messy but easy. When it came time to slice the fish open Mamie had to hold back the bile that was making its way up her throat. Mamie chopped the head and tail off each fish. Then she lay the largest of the catch flat on the ground and slid the knife along the side of the fish length wise. The knife was surprisingly sharp and easily cut though the bones in its way. When Mamie flipped the fish open to expose its guts, she had to close her eyes and hold her breath momentarily. Then she reached inside bare handed and removed the intestine and anything else that she thought she would not want to eat.

When Tyrone returned an hour later Mamie had a small fire going and the fish cooking wrapped in leaves on a large rock in the center of the fire. Tyrone could not hold back a huge smile.

"Well now, you are smarter than you look! But how in the hell did you start the damn fire?"

"I found some matches in the house", Mamie responded, and for the first time in weeks they both laughed together.

This was the beginning of Mamie's mini tactical training. Because of Mamie's growing belly a lot of physical activities were only discussed and repeated over and over until Tyrone felt she had it memorized. He taught her how to hunt, fish, and most importantly to be constantly aware of her surroundings.

Mamie's Mayhem by
The1Essence

Mamie learned the sounds of the Bayou, which snakes were poisonous and how to spot them. She surprised him one day by perfectly peeling a tomato with the 4 inch knife, in front of him.

"Oh shit", he thought to himself.

As Mamie got further along in her pregnancy Tyrone urged her to go to live with one of her sister's out of concern for the unborn child. She didn't speak to him for a week. He never spoke of her leaving again and the breezed through the winter.

The first early spring breeze brought Mamie's labor pains with it. Tyrone was a complete loss as to what to do but she assured him they did not need a hospital and, they could bring her child into the world by themselves.

Mamie's resilience continued to awe Tyrone. He had learned not to challenge her once she set her mind to a goal. Anytime he tried to even slightly force her to change her though process she withdrew from him, most often by wondering off into the bayou for days at a time. His concern for her wellbeing and that of the baby directed him to keep his objections to himself.

Surprisingly, Mamie did not labor long. When she felt the urge to start to push she hobbled outside the shanty to the back of pickup truck with the bewildered Tyrone following behind her. Holding on to the edge of it she squatted and began to push.

"Catch!" Mamie managed to yell at Tyrone in between constipated screams.

Tyrone kneeled down beside her, extending his hands beneath her, and did as the young woman, no longer a child, said. After a few moments that seemed like an eternity to him he felt the top of the child's head emerge.

"Oh my God girl! You doin' it!" Tyrone yelled.

Mamie stopped pushing for a moment to catch her breath. The pain was excruciating. Then with an earsplitting scream Mamie gave a final push. The small pale child fell into Tyrone's hands.

The exhausted Mamie, still gripping the back of the pickup truck, put her head down and relaxed for a brief moment; she thought there may have been another child inside her so she pushed again. The afterbirth materialized and smashed to the ground, Tyrone almost through up as Mamie fell to the ground.

Tyrone handed Mamie the boy child, reached into his back jean pocket and pulled out his switchblade. This part he knew how to do from being present at his daughter's birth. While Mamie sucked the mucus out of the child's nose and mouth, Tyrone cut the umbilical cord of the now screaming baby then settled down on the ground next to her.

"Girl, I have never been so scared in my life", he whispered to the panting Mamie who was trying to get the child to suckle her breast.

"How did you know how to do that? Where did you learn that?" He asked completely confused. Mamie managed a tired laugh.

"Like you said, I am smarter than I look", Mamie answered.

"Well, it looks like we got ourselves a fine, healthy baby boy. What you gon'e call him?"

"Nicolas, Nicolas McGillicuddy after his daddy", Mamie said, then laid her head on his shoulder.

Tyrone crinkled his eyebrows in confusion. He could have sworn the man that sold him this land was named Thaddeus Benton. But, he didn't say a word.

Unbeknownst to the both of them, the pale pink child who was now hungrily sucking his mother's breast bore a striking resemblance to his maternal grandfather, Patrick McGillicuddy.

Two years after the birth of little Nicky, Mamie announced to Tyrone that it was her 18th birthday.

"That calls for a celebration! Why don't we all get into the truck and go to out for pizza in Gulfport?"

"Oh that would be great!" Mamie responded.

In the years since she had given birth Mamie grew more receptive to venturing out with Tyrone. They had become a family with Tyrone taking on the role as father and grandfather. But he knew this announcement signified more than a birthday celebration and, he didn't know whether to be happy that Mamie was easing back into a somewhat normal life or afraid of losing his family. Still, he was even more afraid of what Mamie would do once she was away from his guidance and protection.

Mamie had taken to wondering off for a few days at a time. He had no idea where she went but when she returned she had a wild look and air about her and would insist on more survival training. It often took a couple days for her to return to her normal cheerful, motherly ways.

One month had passed since her last disappearance and Tyrone felt that the next time she left, she wouldn't return. So, he had put little Nick on his back in a carrier he picked up in the city and followed her keeping a bit of distance just in case the child began to cry or chatter.

Mamie had learned from him well. She walked for eight hours straight until reaching her destination, little well-kept cottage outside of New Orleans. Then she watched the four occupants come and go for days, paying particular attention to the elderly woman who sometimes sat alone on the veranda. How she found this place or what she was doing there, Tyrone would never know. He did know, that there was nothing good going to come out of her secret visits.

It was going on two years since Lissette Batiste was murdered and her suspected killer escaped from his police roadblock. No one was talking of it in town anymore. Cutty still held hope that his little sister was alive and out her dreams happily in New York or Chicago. No one could live in a place like this forever. And after everything that she had been through she deserved a little bit of sunshine.

As for him, he was secretly preparing to leave also. He had sold most of his properties and hidden the money in a secret bank account in preparation for his departure. He thought he would wait around for his ageing mother to die. But, she was too stubborn to die. Although, in the last year she had taken to moment of indolence, sitting on the veranda and staring out into the bayou as if she were watching someone or someone was watching her.

How the household was run had changed too. Ruby was now in charge the day to day management of the couple of whores they had left in the stable. And, Rachel was now visibly pregnant with Cutty's child. A feat that was accomplished at the prodding of Nicolette, she needed a grandchild. All of them knew Cutty didn't love Rachel. But none but him seemed to care. The worry and wonderment over

Mamie's disappearance had left him a shadow of the pimp he had been trained to be.

Cutty's days were spent driving around Louisiana looking for any tips on Mamie's disappearance. He actually thought he saw her in Gulfport one spring afternoon but, dismissed the notion as the woman he stared at held a baby and the hand of an older world weary man. That couldn't have been Mamie. In his mind he would find Mamie happy and carefree in a big city. Still he recorded the incident along with his feelings in his journal that evening. The truth of the matter is that he felt guilty. If he had not given Mamie a job, none of this would have ever happened.

For a week Tyrone watched Mamie secretly pack the baby and her things and, some of his. In particular, his seven inch serrated hunting knife. Then the day finally came when Mamie announced that she was taking the baby to Mississippi to see her sisters.

"You need me to carry ya'll up there?" He asked. He knew she was lying.

"Oh no", she answered, "I will get there by myself."

"Mamie, now you know I don't like you hitchhiking. And you gonna take the baby on the road with you? That ain't right." Tyrone fought back tears at the thought of them leaving.

Mamie grew quiet and continued stuffing her duffle with some of the baby's things.

"Now don't get quiet on me. You and Nick leaving and that's that. So, let's not part on a sour note". He told her.

Mamie put down the small baby shoes she was hold and walked over the chair where Tyrone was sitting. Leaning down she hugged him and kissed him softly on the cheek.

"We're leaving tonight." She whispered in his ear. Tyrone got up from the chair and walked out the shanty.

When he came back, just before sunset, Mamie and little Nicolas were gone.

Mamie's Mayhem by
The1Essence

Mamie walked through the bayou with Nick in her arms until she reached the main road. She thought about hitch hiking the rest of the way but heeded Tyrone's warning and kept walking quickly. She had plenty of supplies and time to get to the McGillicuddy cottage. She knew from her secret visits there that Cutty and the pregnant Rachel went to bed around 10pm., then Nicolette would sit on the veranda until Ruby arrived home around midnight. She watched them for days at time to memorize their routine and tonight would be Madam Nicolette's last.

On her last visit, Mamie had erected a tiny lean to in a wooded area just outside the McGillicuddy property line but, close enough for her to still see the occupants move around the house. Mamie was glad to see it so she could feed Nick and catch a little sleep before 10.

10 pm came quickly, Mamie watch the lights turn off one by one until only a small light illuminated from the home. But, tonight Nicolette did not come outside.

"It don't matter", Mamie said out loud to no one, "When it's your time, it's your time". She lifted the sleeping baby, rope and the hunting knife, and started towards the house, leaving the backpack behind. She quietly crept up the veranda steps and when she reached the porch she heard Nicolette voice.

"Come in child. I have been waiting on you. The door is unlocked."

Mamie entered and followed the light into the dimly lit formal room where she found Nicolette sitting in a rocking chair reading the Bible.

"Aren't you supposed to be an atheist or something", Mamie asked her as she set the sleeping baby down on the couch, "When did you get religion?"

"That is not important, don't you think?" Nicolette replied. "Is that my grandchild?" She asked as Mamie bound her hands and feet to the rocking chair. Nicolette didn't resist.

Mamie ignored Nicolette's question and continued to tie square knots in the ropes.

"You don't have to worry child. I won't fight you. I know it is time that I pay penance for my sins."

"I'm not a child anymore. And you will get no penance or mercy from me." Mamie told her.

"As well as I didn't expect any. But, don't you want to know why Ja'miah? I know you do. Anyone in your position would."

Mamie quietly walked into the hall of the old house and picked up a hurricane lamp.

When she returned untitled the turban head wrap the old woman wore and doused it with the lamps kerosene, pouring the remainder on her prisoner's lap. Long, Thick grey plats that fell down to Nicolette's shoulders were released.

"That child is beautiful", Nicolette continued, "but, he will not live long. You are not strong enough to raise a man to live long. But, I supposed that is not your fault but your mother's. She wasn't strong enough to live long either."

Mamie knew she was purposely trying to incite her. But, Mamie would not be detoured from what had taken years for her to plan. But, the mention of Lissette made Mamie's blood boil and she dropped the empty lantern as she stuffed the soaked, putrid head scarf deep into Nicolette's mouth to silence her.

The noise startled the sleeping baby awake and he began to cry loudly. Mamie went over to him to console him then sat him in the middle of the floor and resumed her executioner plans.

The strong smell of kerosene and the cries of a baby woke both Cutty and Rachel. He got out of bed to investigate with Rachel close behind. Rachel screamed when they entered the formal living room and saw Mamie standing behind Nicolette with a knife to her throat. Cutty froze in place as if he were seeing a ghost. Nicolette looked at Cutty with tears in her eyes as if at that moment she decided she didn't want to die.

Only Rachel screamed as both Tyrone and Ruby rushed through the front door. Tyrone had known all the time Mamie was plotting revenge and when he returned to the shanty, he knew where she was going and what she was going to do. He only hoped he could stop her.

Ruby heard the scream as she was opening the door. Tyrone rushed over and picked up the baby off the floor whose screams now joined Rachel's. Ruby just as Cutty was frozen in place watching the horrific scene unfold. Only Tyrone spoke to Mamie.

"Baby, you don't wanna do this. Put the knife down and let's go home. Or, I will take you to your sister's house. But, don't do this." Mamie wasn't listening. The darkness had set in, and would allow nothing to penetrate it.

She was gripping the hunting knife tightly in right hand as she held it firmly against Nicolette's leathered neck, each serration now had a tiny bit of blood oozing down from their tips. A hand full of Nicolette's hair occupied the left hand allowing Mamie to pull her victim's head even further back.

Mamie's mind began to fill with the sight of her mother being nearly decapitated, and the memories of being beaten and raped. Those visions initiated her right hand to move firmly back and forth in a sawing motion across Nicolette's neck. Blood spurt around the room as if it were erupting from a volcano.

When Mamie reached what she felt was bone she began hacking at the neck of the now corpse until she had freed the head of her victim from its body. Then she stretched out her arms, the bloody, dripping knife in one hand and the head of her mother's tormentor in the other, and let out a shrill scream that quieted the screams of everyone watching this grotesque scene play out before them.

When she stopped screaming, Mamie released the knife and the head. Letting both noisily fall to the floor. She looked blankly at Tyrone with tears in her eyes but not one fell.

"Well, if ever there was a time to leave this place I would say ya'll got about 30 seconds to get what you need." Tyrone said to the other witnesses.

Everyone scattered with their own agenda. All Cutty wanted was his journal; the twins ran to their room and began throwing their clothes out the window.

Tyrone eased up on Mamie, putting his free arm around her waist he began to pull her away from the still blood spurting corpse. Halfway across the room he heard Mamie faintly speak.

"What did you say baby", he whispered.

"Www, Wait", was all Mamie could manage to push out.

Tyrone stopped and handed Mamie the baby. He knew what she wanted to do and he knew she wanted to do. But, now he would finish it. As Mamie and the baby both silently watch, Tyrone walked over and picked up his bloody knife and put it in his belt. Slowly, he pulled a book of matches out of his pocket, struck one then used it to light the rest then he tossed the fire on to the blood and kerosene soaked corpse. The smell of burning flesh was atrocious but he had smelled worse.

Tyrone and Mamie watched the corpse burn for a few minutes then he ushered her out of the house, towards the pickup truck.

"Come on Mamie, let's go home…"

Tonight

*Mamie's Mayhem by
The1Essence*

…When Mamie screamed, Nicole almost lost control of her new car. She swerved and barely missed ending up in a ditch.

After pulling on the side of the road and stopping the car, she shook Mamie awake.

"Girl whatchu doin'?" Mamie sleepily asked. Nicole looked at her wide mouth and eyed before you answered.

"Yo' ass need to stop smoking weed! You were having a nightmare! Screamin' and shit like you were losing yo' mind. I almost fucked up my car!"

"Damnnnn, serious? Shit….oh well, I'm woke now bitch. Just drive."

Nicole rolled her eyes and got back on the highway.

"All this killin' got everybody losing their mind and they tryin' to take me with them. Damn!" She said under her breath as she got back on 94 South towards Chicago.

Mamie lay back in her seat, her head spinning from a dream that felt so real. But, then again, if what Cutty Sr. had written in his the notebook Bernoski gave her after he died was more than a novel he was writing…she did live it…

Mamie's Mayhem by
The1Essence

Mamie's Mayhem by
The1Essence

Other
Books by
The1Essence

Mamie's Mayhem by
The1Essence

Available on
www.The1Essence.com

**Available on
www.The1Essence.com**

**Available on
PublishAmerica.com**

*Mamie's Mayhem by
The1Essence*

Reflections of Light
An Extensive Compilation of Poetry
Available on
www.The1Essence.com